# Portal 10

## Speculative Fiction

# Portal 10

## Speculative Fiction

Edited by
Camille Griep

LASCAUX BOOKS

ISBN 10: 0-9851666-7-3
ISBN 13: 978-0-9851666-7-0

Cover design by Grant Willingham and Wendy Russ.
Cover illustration by Bruce Rolff.

Lascaux Books
www.lascauxbooks.com

# Contents

2018 Portal Prize Winner
Family Mart, by Elizabeth Browne ............................................1

Finalists
The Portrait Artist, by Janet Barrow.................................22
Junk, by Christopher Fox...............................................57
Mr. Chips and the Mango-Tango Mother Ship,
by Alice Hatcher...........................................................69
Good Times, by Alexander Jones..................................86
Liberty Motel, by Larry Malchow ...............................104
Sea Change, by Sara Ramey ......................................138
Madrina, by Sara Rivera ............................................161
In a Manner of Speaking, by Charity Tahmaseb.................196
Moon, Flower, Sword, Kendra, by Tom Wharton.............219

Contributors.......................................................... 237

# Introduction

It is said that in times of social strife—unarguably a place we find ourselves in the world regardless of political sway—we turn to the speculative as readers, as listeners, as diners of story. Easy Street's first Portal Prize shines light on fiction that blends the surreal and the mundane, the inconceivable present with the unthinkable future.

Judging fiction contests is never simple. Easy Street's team of readers, writers, and thinkers lovingly tended hundreds of these small infernos of the heart, turning and returning to those tales that left indelible scorches of truth. This collection of stories, culled from so many worthy submissions, is therefore not a final judgement of the worth of these tales, but a roadmap of sorts where X marks the spots we collectively stopped to warm ourselves.

May you do the same.

—Camille Griep

# Family Mart
by Elizabeth Browne

"What's wrong with your arm?" the cashier asks, ringing up Martine's instant noodles, vitamin drinks, and rice crackers and depositing them into a bag. His nametag reads Charoen Wattanapanit and he has a button with a smiley face on it pinned to his Family Mart polo shirt.

"Nothing," she says, but she tugs her left sleeve down, just in case. With her right hand she lifts her items, one-handed and one by one, out of her basket. Her left arm hangs limp at her side. Charoen Wattanapanit smiles, a bright flash of white that Martine knows is a sign of embarrassment but which charms her nonetheless. She's been coming to Family Mart every few nights for nearly a month, and every visit she's greeted by him. Until now he's stuck to the usual pleasantries—"Hello, welcome to Family Mart!" "Thanks for shopping Family Mart!" "Good night!"—and Martine has responded in kind, trying to be polite, but also hoping to avoid any openings in conversation like this. She's reminded of how much her light skin and long blonde hair stand out here, and she's angered by her own carelessness. How could this shopkeeper not notice a tall blonde

1

who appears to have only one working hand; who shops alone in the middle of the night; who speaks fluent Thai; who wears an oversized grey sweatshirt in Bangkok—as if it's Bangor and the trees are changing color? She slides her wallet out of the back pocket of her jeans with her right hand and produces a stack of baht, fixing her expression into what she hopes is an unfriendly mask.

He knows, she thinks. He knows, he knows, he knows.

The cashier presses buttons, counts out change and deposits coins into Martine's outstretched right hand. She closes her fingers around the change and thrusts it into the plastic bag of food on the counter, dropping the coins in among the items inside. When she moves to snatch the bag and escape, he puts his hand on top of the plastic. "My name is Charoen Wattanapanit," he says, in English, then points to his nametag. "You can call me Charo." The smile reappears.

"Nice to meet you," she says in Thai, then turns and strides to the door, whose electronic chime accompanies her out into the night.

For weeks now, Martine has wondered how she ended up this way. One day her left hand held the bar on the Skytrain, steadied her camera, and formed the asdf to her right's jkl;. Now, her wrist has grown a ring of blonde hair, and out of that comes the hoof, gray and waxy. A miniature-pony-sized hoof at the end of her otherwise normal, human arm. She fights its weight. She tries, again and again, to wiggle her lost fingers, but she can only make the hoof bob up and down. The effort shames her.

Bangkok is a throbbing, sweating place. The humidity slows time, or at least Martine used to think that, when she first left the States for Thailand seven years ago. So many expats, and the city feels like an overheated version of home—a moister, less obvious New York.

The foreigners abbreviate; the world is all airport codes and Internet speak. Bangkok is BKK; Kuala Lumpur is KLM. They send text messages and buy sleek cell phones. They start Internet companies that make Martine think of a magician she used to see on the street corner as a child, waving his hands through the air to demonstrate how invisible the rabbit had become. At parties the foreigners tell each other that Asia is now, that America and Europe are so over.

It turns out time slips by just the same in BKK as it does in NYC. Martine wonders how it is that a summer trip turned into a seven-year stay, how seven years can yield only transient relationships that flicker and disappear, screens that go dark. How she can live in a place whose daily temperature is higher than her own. Yet she stays. She is, despite the emptiness, despite the air of superiority of the expats she meets, in awe of the orchids that manage to grow on the cement in the alley behind her apartment building. She's in the habit of strolling the food stalls that mushroom under freeway overpasses, and she joins the Thais that gather there on plastic stools for plates of spiced pork and vegetables that make her pale skin flush and her nose sweat. Mosquitoes dance around bare bulbs. When Martine returns to her apartment, her long blonde hair reeks of chilies and lemongrass.

The hoof is growing. It's been a month, and it lengthens and curls, aching and pressing against the opening of the worn sleeve of Martine's sweatshirt. She runs through the options again and again, then rejects them all again and again. She could meet with a doctor. A vet? She's thought of moving to a hill-country village. She could live more cheaply and in relative isolation, but her foreignness would attract even more attention there. Flying back to New York has its appeal—she feels somehow that she could hide the hoof more easily in that city's brashness. But then she pictures the security scanner at the airport, imagines the agents pointing out the oddity at the end of her human bones. Late at night, amputation begins to sound alluring.

Instead she has been searching the sprawl of Chattuchak Market every Saturday for the tools of a farrier. She has done research online and she knows what she's looking for. It's just a matter of finding someone to sell her what she needs. She can pay.

She calls in sick at the English-language magazine where she has been working as a photographer. After two weeks, when it's clear the hoof isn't going to retreat, she calls again and quits. She tells the magazine's editor she's going home to New York, that she's leaving Bangkok. It happens so often, with so many staff members, he does not sound surprised or concerned. She knows that another *farang* is waiting to take her place. She is expendable. All of the expats here are; temporary, interchangeable, and expendable.

Martine fears revealing her hoof—the hoof—she cannot think of it as a part of her yet. She's terrified of what would happen if someone should catch a glimpse of it, and she stays holed up in her studio for some weeks, grazing on snack food from Family Mart, and talking to the geckos that shriek on the ceiling. She shops in the middle of the night, after the last of the office workers has gone home and even the acrid odors of the temporary restaurants have dissipated. When Charo is on duty.

Two nights later she can tell Charo has been waiting for her. He waves when the door signals her entrance. She wants to turn around and slip back into the Bangkok night, but he waves again and calls out "hello!"

She wears the oversized sweatshirt, the sleeves tugged down distractedly—one over her right hand, and one over the place where her left hand used to be. She's conscious of the hoof always, even after several weeks of its log-like presence at the end of her arm. It looks out of place on her willowy frame, a blunt end to an otherwise graceful physique.

Martine raises her right hand in greeting, then lets it drop to her side. She leans down to pick up a basket and when she stands up, Charo is there, right in front of her. "Welcome back to Family Mart," he says. That smile again.

Martine grimaces. "Thank you." She jams her left arm into the kangaroo pouch on the front of her sweatshirt.

"Can I help you?" Charo points to the basket.

Martine wishes he would go away but doesn't know how to extricate herself without being rude. She hands him the basket and nods.

For a moment they stand in the fluorescent brightness near the doorway. Martine notices Charo is older than she first guessed. She'd assumed he was a teenager, perhaps a university student—Thai youth staffed convenience stores like this all over Bangkok. But there's wisdom around Charo's eyes, and a few grays in his dark hair. His skin is tanned like a laborer's, odd for someone who works in the sunless night. Perhaps he works two jobs, Martine thinks.

"Please," Charo says, gesturing to Martine to go ahead of him down the first aisle.

She's embarrassed by his help, and she walks quickly, head down, past the bags of snack chips. She cannot remember what she wanted to buy.

"Excuse me, miss," Charo says in English. He bends down and produces a package of rice crackers. The same ones Martine has been buying on previous visits. She nods her consent, and he deposits them in the basket, looking pleased.

They continue in this way down the instant noodle aisle. Charo remembers all of her preferences. Martine cannot seem to speak. After they have gone through all of the packaged foods, Charo points to a refrigerated case. "Would you like some juice?" he asks. "Or iced coffee?"

He holds the sliding glass door open for her, and she selects some juices, milk, a few oranges, a Japanese yogurt brand she particularly likes.

They walk to the cash register together, and Charo leaps over the counter. He vaults like a gymnast, muscled and quick.

Charo puts Martine's food in a bag as he has on every other night. He holds out her change with two hands—Thai custom—and though it may seem rude to him, she accepts it with only her right hand, first the change, which she dumps into the bag, then the bills, which she stuffs into her back pocket. She no longer bothers with a wallet. Later she

6

will empty the contents of the plastic bag on her bed and pick up each item, then the coins, one by one, and in this way, with this chore, some part of the night would pass more quickly.

"Well," she says, her hand on the bag. "Thank you for your help."

"It's my pleasure," Charo says. As he does so, he nods at her arm, the lump in the pouch on her front. She's almost been able to forget about it in these few awkward minutes with a stranger in the middle of the night. Realizing that the stranger was aware of it always, she panics, snatches the bag from the counter, and spins toward the door. "Good night," she says, not looking back.

As the door chimes in her wake, she hears Charo call out in English, "What is your name?"

Since the hoof appeared, Martine has considered each of the friends and acquaintances she's made in Bangkok. Co-workers and former co-workers, Thais and *farangs*. Before the hoof she might have counted any number of them as confidantes, but now she can't think of one she trusts enough to share her new extremity with. Her ex-boyfriend Mark? She's remained close to the New Zealander—he teaches English at the university in Phra Nakhon—but she can't bring herself to give him a call. She begins to see her time in Bangkok as out of time altogether. How is it possible to live somewhere for so long and yet have nothing—no one—to show for it?

Martine wonders whether the replacement of her hand was painful, whether she blacked out when her fingers turned to gelatin. She can't remember anything that might explain the arrival of the hoof. One night she possessed a working collection of bones and joints and tissue, a life line and a love line, fingerprints, and half-moons for nails. The next morning all that identity had solidified into a horny lump.

She mourns the shape of her nails, her ragged cuticles, those whorls of prints. She cannot stop the dreams in which her left hand returns, full of motion and dexterity. She types; she grips a plate of *gai pad khing* while her right hand holds a spoon; she's driving a car, hands on the wheel at 10 and 2, just like they tell you to; she's taking photos, her left hand steadying the camera and adjusting the lens while she controls the shutter with her right. The worst dreams are the ones in which someone—she can't make out his face— joins her in a double bed, and she slides two electric hands over his skin.

It is Saturday again, and Martine weaves through Chattuchak Market's cramped stalls, past antique Buddha statues, bootlegged DVDs, bright bolts of silk. She nudges past tourists ogling puppies sluggish from the heat. The hoof is now too long for her sleeve to conceal, so that she has to keep her left arm safely tucked into the kangaroo pocket on the front of the sweatshirt, a tube sock pulled over the end, just in case. Just when she believes she's covered all 35 acres of stalls, she discovers another alley that leads to more. The heat on the corrugated roofs is unbearable, but she presses through the crowds, sweating, skin flushed.

The weeks of solitude make the normalcy of life around her seem untouchable and faraway, as if behind glass. Her pale eyes dart about and her hair is unbrushed. The hoof's constant growth and heavy pulseless weight at the end of her arm are creating a kind of claustrophobia in her. She has tried working at the hoof wall with scissors but it resists, and the scissors leave odd markings, like graffiti carved into the trunk of a tree.

She has been avoiding Family Mart, and the aromas from the food stalls make her feel weak. Even the Thai snacks she dislikes—quail eggs, fried fish cakes, silkworm larvae—look appetizing. She knows she is losing weight and the force of her hunger pulls her to a satay seller's cart. Martine feels a surge of confidence that she'll be able to eat the meat from the skewer there in the bustle of the market with just one hand. She offers her money to the man and for an awkward moment the seller waits for her to take the skewer, but Martine cannot until the money is removed from her outstretched right hand. Finally, the seller, scowling, lays the skewer on a napkin, then takes her money. Satay secured, Martine sits on a plastic chair in the shade. She is dying to take off the sweatshirt. She wears a miniskirt and flip-flops to compensate for the bulk on her upper body, but still she's overheated. Her bare feet are black with grime. The meat tastes good, and she remembers the freshness of the food stalls in her neighborhood, misses the old ladies who stir-fry more chilies into her *gai pad kaprow* because she is "colorless" and add more rice to her plate because they think she is too thin.

At first Martine thinks she is imagining him. I've been alone for too long, she thinks, look at me, now I'm dreaming of the convenience store cashier. But as she sets the half-eaten skewer of pork on her bare thigh and wipes her mouth with a napkin, she is sure of it; Charoen Wattanapanit sits at a nearby table with an older man. They lean toward each other, speaking in low tones and taking long, serious drags on cigarettes. Brows furrowed, teeth bared. The older man's hair has receded and is gray over his ears. He is sun-creased and thin, his bony feet exposed in the cheap plastic flip-flops Thais often wear. Like Charo, he is dark-skinned, like a laborer. The older man stands so abruptly the stool he was sitting on tumbles to the ground behind him. He stubs out his cigarette on the table and barks something at Charo, then turns and marches past a teenage girl selling grilled octopus from a hibachi cart. The smoke swirls in his wake for a moment and then Martine blinks and the man has vanished into the market.

Martine concentrates on the skewer again, eyes down, hoping to avoid a potential meeting with the convenience store cashier and his curiosity. When she tears at the meat, juices from the pork run down the crease in her palm to her wrist, and she licks at the heel of her hand. On the other side of the eating area she sees Charo rise, toss his butt to the dust underfoot, and follow in the direction of the older man. Almost as if there was a timing to it, Martine thinks, as she returns her gaze to the skewer, as if he meant to give the old man a head start.

Martine pauses for a moment by the food sellers' carts, then chooses an opening in the stalls to resume her search. She shimmies past tourists haggling over baseball caps and knock-off jeans, past Thai housewives buying spices whose colors make her think of dried grass and fall leaves. With each step the goods seem to rise higher, closer to the roof. Sneakers tangle around a pole, wool blankets dangle from rafters. The pathways between vendors narrow. Bolts of fabric are packed into shelves that rise to the corrugated plastic roofing in walls of color. Martine scans tables strewn with lacquerware and hammers, kitchen knives and rolls of tape. Glass jars of saffron threads look like bottled flames.

The crowds begin to thin, and the smells of curry and roast pork give way to those of fish guts and the tang of salt water. Martine steps over a bucket of writhing eels. The fishy odor is heavy and she cups her free hand over her nose and mouth. She sidles around tubs of snails and sea cucumbers and anchovies, tries to avoid puddles and hoses. In the heat, the remaining fish barely move. The fresh catch goes early, before the animals begin to suffocate in their makeshift tanks. Some of the stalls are dark—the day's catch long since sold—and the vacant space in the normally crowded market makes Martine feel uneasy. She's alone, save for a few men in waders smoking and spraying down buckets and pallets. One flashes stained teeth at her and she catches the word *farang* in his banter with the others. The word "foreigner" suddenly contains a hint of menace. She walks faster.

At the end of the aisle, an open courtyard. In contrast to the empty seafood vendors' stalls, it's loud and bright. A throng of Thai men are gathered around a cement pit, yelling and jeering. The sun is unrelenting. It's a common area of sorts, with aisles of the market radiating out from this hot center. Martine can hear the desperate squawking of birds and her arm throbs in its pouch, straining for release. She pushes her way into the crowd. Because she is foreign and the only woman the men give her space; because they are entranced by the cockfight they do not hold their stares

11

for long. Those at the edge of the pit yell the loudest, clutch their tickets. The gamecocks squeal. The birds are huge, standing up to Martine's knees perhaps, and they wear spurs taped to their legs like thorns. They've become feathered fiends, claws extended, on the attack.

A shirtless man touches her arm and shakes his head. When he opens his mouth to speak, Martine smells betel and sees the places where his teeth used to be. "You shouldn't be here," the man says. "Women are bad luck." The squeals and squawks of the birds grow louder. Martine backs away from the old man's breath and superstitions. When she looks into the ring again, one of the roosters bleeds from a wound on his breast. There's a glinting on the other side of the pit, where the men are jeering and shaking their fists, and Martine sees the curved blade of a knife hanging from a belt. She fights panic. It's the heat and their exposed chests and stained teeth, the peaceful reduced to the primal. The hoof. Martine knows she should leave, get herself into a more touristed area of the market, that this is the kind of intuition guidebooks say to heed.

But in the sun and the press of bodies and the smell of birds and blood, she is unable to look away. The crowd roars with every shriek and flap of feathers. The men spit betel and push closer and closer to the pit. The winning cock hovers above the ground for a moment before lunging at his opponent a last time. Its wings spread in a flash of vermillion and gold. Then there's a piercing squeal and a spray of blood. Martine closes her eyes.

That's when she hears his pleading cries on the other side of the pit; knows she's been hearing them all the while. She turns to the sound: Two men hold Charoen Wattanapanit's arms behind his back, and he is straining to get free. "Let him go! Let him go!" he yells. Two others have pinned the older man against a cement wall, and they are hitting him, punching him. There's blood around his mouth and he sags under the hands that hold him up.

Martine pushes through the heat and the smell of too-close bodies. The spectators, distracted by their sport, or wise enough not to get involved, do not meet her eyes as they let her through.

"I'll pay you!" Charo shouts, and still the thugs are on the old man.

Martine is aware that this is not the way, that a one-handed, one-hoofed *farang* is an oddity, not a savior, but she's not going to stop, she has nothing to lose. Her right hand is a fist, and for the first time since she ate she realizes the satay skewer is still in it, has somehow become a part of her hand, like a weapon.

When he sees her, Charo stops struggling, and his sudden lack of resistance causes the men to look in her direction. They are thick bulging men, the kind Martine sees driving BMWs rather than tiny Korean cars or sputtering mopeds. She's always felt vaguely nervous about passing these types on the street, and now she knows why.

"Let them go," Martine says in Thai, her voice even and faraway. Her heart hammers. She feels it has risen to the base of her neck. Wonders if being a red-faced blonde will be enough of a distraction.

"Who's this, your girlfriend?" one of the men says to Charo with a creepy smile that reveals gold teeth and pointed incisors. He's the leader, Martine understands, and the others his entourage. He nods, and his bodyguards stop punching the old man and push Charo free. Charo says nothing, does not intimate that he has any idea who she is.

One of them points to Martine's fist. "What's she going to do, attack us with her toothpick?" More laughter.

Charo looks at Martine, and then, perhaps ashamed, at the ground. His face reveals nothing, but his shoulders slump and he relaxes his fists. The old man crouches against the wall, sweating in the sun, his eyes closed, his chest rising and falling.

Martine considers pulling the sock-covered hoof from its pouch, and slamming it into the side of the gold-toothed man's head. Instead she drops the skewer and turns to the old man. Leans down to speak to him. "Come on," she says, "I'll help you get out of the sun."

His eyes fly open, alarmed perhaps, but he says nothing and allows her to lean down awkwardly so that she can put her good arm under his and pull him to his feet. She's conscious of the four men laughing still, the leader calling over his shoulder to Charo, "We'll come back for you, bird shit."

The cock fighting has resumed and the clamor around the ring grows louder again. The old man limps and mutters as Martine helps him into the shade under the market roof. She settles him onto a wooden palette in one of the darkened stalls.

"Papa," Charo begins when he joins them. He looks as though he wants to say more but closes his mouth and stares at the ground. There are angry marks on his arms where the men held him. Martine cannot believe this is the same man who beams at her in Family Mart, who exudes cheer and vaults over counters. He looks defeated and broken.

"You owe them money?" Martine says, forgetting to swallow her American directness.

His face transforms when he smiles, and whatever tension he carried seems to rise, untethered, into the city's haze. It's a smile of embarrassment though, not graciousness. "My father—" he gestures to the older man, who is looking better already, as if a beating by local thugs is a normal part of his day. He's craning to see the action in the ring. "Gambling debts."

"I'm sorry," Martine says, though she is not sure what it is she is sorry for, or even if she is disappointed.

Charo's father struggles to his feet. "This is going to be a good match," he says, pointing to the ring. "Old Mongkut's fighting a winner."

"Papa, we need to leave now. You know they'll be back."

"Bah! I can put a dent in the account with this one," Charo's father says, waving a hand at his son as if to brush aside his concerns. He gives a nod to Martine, and limps over to the crowd.

Charo shakes his head. The crinkles at the corners of his eyes that Martine had seen as evidence of his unassailable cheer now seemed etched from obligation and disappointment.

"You work at night to pay your father's debts," she says, the realization coming as she speaks it.

He nods. "And you, why are you awake in the middle of the night?"

Martine scans his face. She jams her left arm into the pouch as far as it can go. She feels sweat rolling through her hair, tastes it on her upper lip.

"Let me see your hand," Charo says.

15

The men roar—something has happened in the cock-fight. "Hurry," he says. "They'll be done soon."

Martine scans the crowd and realizes Charo is right—no one will notice her here. The stakes are too high.

She stares at Charo, her blue eyes hard, and the events of the previous weeks flicker in her thoughts—awakening with this unfamiliar appendage, and then retreating from everything. She takes in Charo's angular cheekbones, his kind eyes, the thickness of his hair.

Martine drags her right sleeve across her mouth. She's shaking.

Then she pulls her left arm out of the pouch and peels back the sock.

Charo's face registers nothing, but he gestures to her to cover up. She slides the sock back over the hoof and jams her arm into her pouch.

"You will come to Family Mart tonight?" Charo says, as much a demand as a question, and she nods.

The men by the ring spit, laugh and exchange money. The winning bird shrieks as he is returned to a wicker cage. A bare-chested man grips the loser by its yellow legs. The bird's neck sliced, blood dripping to the hardened ground below.

As she turns to leave, Charo calls out. *Khaap kun krap.* Thank you.

Back in her apartment that night, Martine undresses, wrestling with the sweatshirt to extricate herself from it with only one hand. In the shower she squirts shampoo on the top of her head, then massages it in with her right hand. For the first time she takes care to lather the hoof. She scrubs it with a brush she uses to clean the tile and feels pleased when the hoof wall squeaks under her fingertips.

After toweling off, she dons a pair of shorts, then reaches for a tank top to wear under the sweatshirt. The sweatshirt lies in a heap on the bathroom tile and when she retrieves it she smells the day—the many days she's worn it. It reeks of grilled meat and tamarind, sweat and exhaust. She looks at it for a moment, then flings it into the corner by the shower nozzle. Impatience and rage spread from the hoof through her body and the nozzle is in her hand and set to "jet." She aims for the gray lump of cotton terry. It shrivels, hit, and a darkness spreads outward.

Outside, the humidity lingers still, and there is the smell of garbage in the street. Family Mart's lime green and blue sign blares into the darkness. A stray dog lies near the door. Already Martine can smell the sausages, fish cakes, and shrimp burgers that broil under the heat lamps by the register. She jogs toward the store, her flip-flops smacking the asphalt.

The dog watches, ears alert, as Martine steps into the air-conditioning. She halts just inside: the fluorescent brightness reminds her that she can no longer hide under the sweatshirt, that she's traded it for a tank top. Her left hoof shines after its cleaning, though the wall is still long, cracked and curled. The smell of food gnaws at her, and she can't help but make her way toward it and place her right hand on the glass of the case where the sausages are spinning and the shrimp burgers slide over hot rollers. Charo is emptying a box of cigarette cartons behind the counter, and he turns around, smiling, to let her know that he knows she's there. When he sees her, he stops. Martine does not miss the quick flash of alarm at her exposed hoof, then the careful rearrangement of his features. He puts the carton of Krong Thips he's holding back into the box on the floor. Martine raises her left hoof thinking that she might wave with it; instead she puts the sole of the hoof to the palm of her right hand and bows in an attempt at the traditional Thai greeting. Charo puts his palms together and bows back. The *wai* is more graceful with hands than hooves, Martine thinks, and at the grief she feels at not being able to put her hands together, such a simple gesture—she begins to cry.

They sit on the floor in aisle two, among the rows of snack chips. Charo brings her the shrimp burger she was coveting. It's wrapped in foil, and he kneels down next to her and peels back the wrapping, then holds it to her lips.

Still her tears come, but the food is irresistible. She does not object when Charo pulls a bottle of green tea from the case, twists the top and holds it up for her to drink. Thai pop music plays over the loudspeakers and Martine lets the lyrics run together and disappear as she swallows.

When she's finished the sandwich, Charo wipes her mouth with a napkin, then dabs away leftover tears from the corners of her eyes. He picks out a brush from the beauty aisle and carefully removes the tangles from her hair.

"Just a moment," Charo says, then disappears into the back of the store. Martine hears the clang of metal on metal. When he returns he has a small, frayed duffle bag slung over one arm. "I brought some tools to take care of your hoof," he says, as he unzips the bag and pulls out a pair of nippers, a hammer and chisel, and a rasp and lines them up on the floor. Martine has been scouring Chattuchak for tools she might have found at any good hardware store and she understands suddenly that her crisis was not the tools she could not find but rather the lack of a partner to wield them.

"Can you help me?" she whispers.

Charo drops to his knees in front of Martine and puts out his hand.

She begins to shake all over. The fact that she can't control her body mortifies her, and she looks down at her pale knees. Charo lifts her hoof gently into the palm of his hand. Then he traces the thin wisps of hair where flesh meets gelatin. He turns her arm over and examines the bottom of her hoof, the soft tissue that forms a "V" down the center, the almost-imperceptible white ring that hugs the outer wall. He runs his fingers down the front of the wall to the point where it curves longer and splits.

Martine closes her eyes. It's been a long time since she's been this close to another human being. Charo's face is too near; she feels dizzy and tries to take a deep breath. As if he senses her discomfort, he stands quickly and heads toward the brightness of the drink cases. Martine feels the absence of his touch on her arm, right at the place where touch dissolved into the unfeeling wall of the hoof.

Charo returns with a can of iced coffee, which he pops open and gulps quickly. Martine tries to remember why everyone she's known in Bangkok seemed so distant, so unknowable. Charoen Wattanapanit is here, she thinks. His presence reminds Martine of some life she knew before Thailand. She feels comfortable with him—a sense that he will not, like others she's known in this country, disappear. She reaches for something to say about the men in the mar-

19

ket that afternoon, how she understands his troubles, but she cannot risk shaming him. She settles for an offering of sorts: "My name is Martine."

"Martine," Charo says, and he kneels, sets his empty can on the floor by the rasp, and puts both hands on her shoulders. "Those men, they come here sometimes, to Family Mart."

She searches his face, the gentleness around around his eyes, and she can't tell if he's worried for her or if he's asking for help, for money. It doesn't matter. She's flooded with relief at being invited into a predicament that has nothing to do with being a *farang* with a hoof. She shrugs in the way that Thais often do, as if to say there's nothing to be done.

Charo sits back and drops his arms to his sides, looking relaxed for the first time since the door chimes signaled her arrival. They both look to the tools on the floor.

"Do you know how to trim it?" Martine asks. Images fly through her head: The ruthlessness of the thugs in the market, their punches, the red-hot metal of horseshoes being forged and nails that pound them into place, blood. She is in this now, too.

"Don't worry," Charo says, picking up her hoof. He lays the sole flat against his upper leg. He pinches the nippers to mark the place where he would cut away the hoof's growth, then he presses the handles together. Snip. Charo glances at Martine to make sure he isn't causing any pain. After he trims the excess growth away, he files the rough edge of the wall with the rasp. Soon waxy shavings appear on his jeans, but he keeps filing, moving the rasp around the half circle of hoof with care. Martine can see the hoof growing shorter and more rounded. She feels as if she's getting a haircut; she's surprised by her anticipation of how the hoof will look when Charo is finished. He draws the rasp across the now-rounded edge of the hoof wall a final time, then sets the instrument on the floor. Then he picks up the hoof and holds it in both hands, as if considering its weight. The sight of them, neatly folded around her newly trimmed hoof, makes Martine's breath catch in her throat.

"Family Mart" originally appeared in *Unstuck*.

# The Portrait Artist
## by Janet Barrow

For three years in my early thirties, I worked in the deli section of a gourmet grocery store. The type of place where a jar of mayonnaise cost fourteen dollars and, though employees got a twenty percent discount on all items, the irony of trading an hour and a half's wages for a six-ounce bottle of hot sauce was never lost on any of us. We sold grass-fed organic beef cuts and sternly odorous cheeses, tapenades and hand-rolled truffles, all without ever indulging a two-dollar bite. We perfected the common language of the products and their consumers, though the products, to us, were nothing more than images.

"Which do you recommend, the Aji Chile Sour Dill pickles or the Brooklyn Brine organics?"

"Well, the Brines are actually steeped in a Dogfish Head sixty minute IPA for three days before packaging, so they've got a really rich and unusual hoppy flavor. They're great if you're a little adventurous, but I personally love a pickle with a classic kick that'll clear your sinuses, so I'd always go for the Chile Sours."

When I spoke this way, I often felt like a puppet on strings, with someone else maneuvering my mouth, extracting my speech. I didn't recognize my voice, but for that, I was grateful. Such is the dual life.

*

When I was thirteen, I attended the birthday party of one of my classmates, Julia, whose J was pronounced in the

German manner, like a Y. It was a traditional young girls' party. We had pizza and cake. Gifts were jealously given, and then we gossiped and played games until it was time for bed. Julia's mother had spread blankets and pillows all over the living room floor, and close friends scrambled to sleep beside one another. I ended up, much to my dismay, sharing a pillow with a pungent little red-headed girl named Minnie.

Even at that age, I was not so cruel or shallow that I would dislike somebody for giving off a rank odor or having a face so spotted you couldn't tell if it were pimples on skin or skin on pimples. But this Minnie—there was always something sinister about her. You might be sitting in class and feel a set of eyes on your back and, without fail, when you turned around, Minnie would be boring into you, her eyes so blue they seemed empty of content. I even swore one time, when a boy fell off the swing set and got considerably bloodied up, that I saw a smile twitch across her lips.

For an hour or so, Minnie and I tried to sleep back to back. Then, I guess in some half-asleep stupor, I turned to face her. In the strangest moment, I opened my eyes only to find her empty gaze fixed upon me. I jerked awake.

"What are you looking at?" I whispered angrily.

"Julia's mom is a painter," she replied.

"And? So what," I spat back.

"I heard she paints pictures of naked ladies, and men too. You can see their *things* in her paintings."

"Yeah, right," I said, sighing and beginning to roll back away from her.

"I found them myself, earlier tonight. I snuck off for a bit."

"Sure you did, Minnie," I quipped.

"Well if you don't believe me, then come with me, and I'll show you. Unless, that is, you're too scared."

I, of course, couldn't let her get away with such blasphemy. I was quite proud for my age, a characteristic I am happy to say slipped off of me a few years later. That night, however, it made me recklessly stubborn. So we climbed, muscles tensed, out of our blankets. We stepped carefully between the splayed limbs surrounding us, and Minnie led us down a hall, past the kitchen, to a door on the left.

"In there," she said, gesturing to the closed door.

I looked at her, her face twisted into a mocking grimace, and then I grabbed the door handle and twisted it firmly to the right. I was unprepared for what was inside. Hundreds of paintings, all of naked men and woman, some with rippling musculature, some with bony limbs and distended bellies, some pregnant, or old and wrinkled, black as charcoal, albino, some with rolls that poured over one another like a thick batter. Somehow, even with such a mix of bodies I found singularly to be ugly, grotesque, beautiful, or altogether frightening, in every painting they managed to be draped into such a configuration that I was never repelled. Instead, I was captivated. Each image absorbed me more than the last.

"Hey, look at this," Minnie said, pulling me back into reality.

"Those are her paints and brushes and everything."

When I looked to where she was pointing, a sudden urge washed over me.

"Let's paint each other," I whispered, almost too quiet to be heard.

"What!" she exclaimed in a cat-like hiss. "Like ... *them*?"

"Yeah, like them," I answered slowly, as though I were just trying the words on for fit.

"But they're all naked."

Suddenly, the thing I had found so off-putting about Minnie fell away. She seemed nervous but excited, like any young girl would be when considering, for a sparkling moment, doing something that she is certain she should not do.

"Well ... so what?" I replied hesitantly. "It'll just be for art. Not for any ... gross reasons."

"Hmmm, I guess," she said, pensively.

"Then," she continued after a long pause, "you have to go first. I mean, I'll paint you first."

*

Facing the door so that my back was turned towards Minnie, I slowly peeled away my clothing. When I finished, I turned to look at her, embarrassed. I still had the body of a two-by-four plank of wood. Not the faintest trace of a hip, no fat to round out the base of my belly. She looked tentatively at my figure, and then we both began to giggle.

"Pose like that one," she said, pointing to a painting propped against the wall behind me. It was of a middle age woman in a sort of straight-backed fetal position. One arm stretched up, forming a cohesive line with her spine, and the other fanned down towards her knees at about a thirty-degree angle to her slight chest, her loose neck. I tried to imitate her, but I'm sure I looked all wrong, with huge gaps and sharp angles in all the places her flesh nicely filled itself in, pressing into and folding over itself self-referentially.

The floor felt cold and unfamiliar against my naked body. Every few minutes, when the silence got to be too much, we'd both start to giggle.

It took Minnie about thirty minutes to finish her portrait of me. I looked at it, and we both burst out laughing. It was a very amateur painting, two-dimensional, with no shadows or variations in the skin tone. It reminded me of pictures I had seen of cave drawings in New Mexico.

Now it was my turn. Minnie was less awkward about undressing than I had been. Probably because she was somewhat of an early bloomer, and proud of it. Her pink nipples had already begun to widen and spread, and there were little creases forming below the slight curve of her breasts. Though her hips were still very square, fat was beginning to gather in layers over her thighs and belly. A few hairs had even sprouted on her pubic mound. I was captivated.

The strangest thing, I realized, was that Minnie's areolas were bigger than my mother's thumb-nail pair. Until that moment, I had imagined that adult bodies functioned via a sort of template, and that height and weight variation was only a stretching, shortening, compressing, or suctioning, of the "original"—the average, if you will. So I was surprised that Minnie, whose breasts were much smaller than my mother's, had larger nipples, and that her nipples even seemed to point marginally outwards, while my mother's sat in a perfect line facing the front.

I began to paint. I started with faint outlines of shapes I found in her body, and then I shaded them in, moving around by groupings of skin colorings and tone, rather than going body part to body part. After a while, Minnie got restless. She was posed standing up, and her legs were getting tired. The magic had worn off. She wanted to go back to sleep.

"Just a little longer," I kept insisting, "I've almost got this part of your foot right."

But eventually, she would be kept no longer. She got dressed and went back to bed.

*

In early September, a little more than five years ago, a man of about sixty-five walked into the deli. I turned to apprehend him at the sound of the automated two-tone bell—like one of Pavlov's dogs. He bore a rounded belly typical of men of his age. He was tall but not overly so—perhaps six feet even, and with a full head of stark white hair. In a dreamy moment, I thought he could have been a brother to my father. But old white men have always seemed to me to boast more similarities—both of physique and general worldly mindset—than differences. It is not at all difficult for me to imagine them all as members of some hugely-overpopulated, too powerful for its own good, family from southwestern Connecticut.

The man approached the counter absently, scanning the refrigerated cheeses from afar. Then, quite suddenly, he looked at me and stopped short.

"Can I help you?" I asked.

"Yes," he said, "I um…"

He paused to clear his throat.

"I um…" he repeated, "just a moment."

Then, strangely enough, he turned and walked away from the counter towards the shelved goods on the other side of the room. I watched him surreptitiously for five minutes while he pretended to examine the labels on boxes of truffle-oil infused crackers and cricket-dust granola bars ("The food of the future!"). He looked anxious, like he'd just launched into a strenuous internal debate. And every few seconds, he flicked his gaze from whatever ingredient list he'd been investigating to glance nervously in my direction.

Growing uneasy myself, I decided to approach him.

"Do you need help finding anything, Sir?" I asked, intent on alerting him through the severity of my tone that I wouldn't be putting up with any nonsense.

He jumped slightly at the sound of my voice.

"Yes," he started, "I was looking for a um … a …"

He shifted from left foot to right.

"Actually, I guess I've forgotten what I was looking for," he concluded.

"Is everything alright?" I ventured.

"Oh yes, yes, I'm sorry. Everything is fine. It's just … well, to be completely honest … it's just that you look so exactly like somebody I knew many years ago."

\*

Before the episode with Minnie, I'd tried painting just one other time—a famous picture of Twiggy wearing a cashmere sweater. I'd pulled it off the internet because my mother was interested in fashion at that time, and therefore I was, or believed that I was, as well. One of her eyes came out much wider than the other, and I turned her slight smile the wrong way, so that she looked scornful instead of playful. And I forgot to give her bottom eyelashes. Characteristic of my young self, the failure to succeed instantaneously represented an end point to me. I dropped the idea of becoming an artist and walked away.

But after Minnie left me alone in Julia's mother's studio, something strange happened. I hadn't, I suddenly knew, been dissatisfied with the painting of Twiggy because of my formal mistakes. Rather, I'd been dissatisfied because I'd been working from a pre-existing image—another artist's image; the photographer's rendering. I'd been trying to paint a subject through a pane of blurred glass. And this time, when I'd looked at Minnie, despite being fascinated, her form, too, had been a deception and a distraction. She had transformed herself into an object, tried to manipulate my perception through her presentation, rather than simply *being*.

Now that I was alone, though, the night stretched long before me. There was no longer any intermediary between me and my brush. Later, I would remember this moment as a sort of initiation; a taking in. I painted until the sun had moved high into the sky, and as the light transformed, so did I, becoming what I have remained to this day—a subjectless painter of portraits.

*

"Just exactly like her," he reiterated.

"Oh?" I replied, taken aback by this strange resolution to his behavior.

"I mean, the resemblance is absolute. You're a perfect facsimile of her circa 1975. Down to the haircut and oversized corduroys. It's kind of knocked the wind out of me," he finished, laughing nervously.

During this period, my hair was cut in quite a severe, if uncommon, style. I wore my bangs short across my forehead, perhaps half an inch in length, and where they terminated, the strands cascaded sharply to just below my earlobe, where the rest of my hair described, at this length, a perfect semi-circle about the back of my head.

I wondered at her having had the same haircut over forty years ago.

"Actually, we were very much in love for most of the 70s." He glanced at the floor embarrassedly, and his cheeks filled with blood.

I nodded tentatively, trying to decide whether he was making an advance.

"Go on."

"For five years, we lived together in this tiny studio apartment in alphabet city—with a rat infestation."

I chuckled with assurance. Talking about rats was not a man's way of being sexy. Seeing that I'd eased up, he began to speak more freely.

"After the hundredth attempt to kill them off, she decided it would be easier to just accept them as part of our lives," he laughed. "She called them our ugly babies. Five years we fell asleep listening to them scratching at the walls."

"So what happened?"

"Didn't work out. For the longest time, the love was electric. Totally magnetic. But then," he drifted off, "well, that's life, isn't it? Things get in the way."

I nodded as though I understood, though I'm not sure I did. I'd never had a love I would call electric.

"And where is she now," I asked tentatively.

"Oh, I don't know. We got in contact a few years back. She's married now. Two sons. Still living in New York City when we talked on the phone. But that must've been ... I don't know, ten years ago."

A distant look precipitated in his eyes, and he grew quiet.

"Anyway..." he mumbled, plunging his hands into his pockets in preparation for departure.

"Could I ask you a question before you go?"

"Sure," he said.

"What was her name?"

"Ah," he breathed, a hint of a smile twitching back across his upper lip, "Claudia. Claudia Rilling."

*

After Minnie, I became a ferocious painter. Painting, for me, is a process of closing in. Day after day, I circle canvas as a lion circles its prey. I trace my wrist in every direction, enclosing my elusive subject with strands of burnt sienna, raw umber, and ochre. And then, with a feverish stroke, always at an unexpected moment, a chance opportunity, I dart forth to wring my subject by the neck. In later years, I came to refer to this moment as "the catch." The catch could otherwise be understood as a recognition, for I never begin a painting with a subject, and I never finish without one. My subjects are unknown to me up until the catch, though they always reveal themselves to be the people that have populated my life, in one capacity or another. My mother and friends, a fisherman I met under a bridge on a still morning, people who stole my blood—doctors and nurses, boyfriends and lovers, but also people who only sold me bread from little kiosks, or who I made prolonged eye contact with on subway cars.

Their recognition takes the form of a capturing, for in recognition, I gain a sense of possession. Before the catch, paintings belong to my unknown subjects. I only swarm them longingly. But after, subject and painting both become mine. When caught, I always know my subjects, even if we only ever met with a handshake at a crowded party. And then, all that is left is the final devouring. The most succulent part of the process, for I am able to gorge at last. I do not need to be silent and slow and careful once my subject is known. I need only gobble them to completion, taste them and let them nourish me with needed fats and proteins, with blood that runs thick and oily down my greedy jowls.

Painting, for me, has always been a strange eroticism.

\*

When I recounted my interaction with the man at the deli to my mother the next day, she had the same reaction as most everybody else would for years to come.

"Just an old man trying to make an impression on a pretty young woman. Creative, I'll give him that."

"But you should've seen the way he reacted when he walked into the store. Like I was the ghost of Christmas past," I argued, sympathetic to my mother's suspicions, but certain that this interaction had been, purely and truly, a singular exception to the bullshit of cat-callers and company.

"Star-struck. You know what a beauty you are, love. I stand by it. Star-struck, and a good actor to-boot. I know you're not easy to fool. But that's the folly of women. Even the smart ones sometimes get swept up in the nonsense of smooth-talkers."

Still, I was convinced that the old man had been telling the truth.

I thought about the experience for a long while. The sensation of standing before him—a memory come to life. In retrospect, it had been quite bewildering. To him, I was not a reality. I was a figment of the past that he'd somehow bumped into at the grocery on an overcast Sunday morning. Standing before him, I opened the floodgates to a gushing of memories, some of which had perhaps become flattened and inaccessible in the interim between seeing her then and seeing her again, now, in me. I'd given life to fossils and ghosts while to me he'd only buzzed like static, a stranger through and through. I felt stripped and penetrated, though not violated. Throughout the time we'd spoken, I hadn't, after all, been me. Instead, I'd been the Claudia Rilling of 1975. A version of me that predated my existence by eight years. The sensation was altogether anomalous.

*

Between the ages of thirteen and fifteen, the peak of my fascination with my mother as a means of understanding femininity, or perhaps, more to the point, the peak of my desire to possess and exude a 'correct' femininity myself, my mother emerged on canvas, again and again, in shades of pink and gold.

In retrospect, this is laughable. My mother is far from the classic picture of delicate "femininity." She is unreserved, bold, occasionally even hot-tempered. Though she is compulsive about some things—the curtains must always be drawn at nine pm sharp, her duvet must always be pulled taught, its corners folded military style, and not a day in her life has she slept past eight in the morning—her rituals have always been her own. She's never seen her own systems of order as universally necessary, and, when I was young, she never took issue with the fact that I made my own bed only about once a month, and, on weekends, often slept until midday. And though she requires order in some parts of her life, in other parts, she is altogether uninhibited. She has, for example, absolutely no need or regard for polished table manners. If we are out to eat somewhere and her legs feel restless beneath the table, she has no problem crossing them into a pretzel beneath her or propping them on the chair beside her. And social nervousness is a distant myth to her. If she is standing in line at the bank and something funny occurs to her, she'll easily turn to the stranger beside her and relay it to them. In all, I think the most interesting thing about her is that, unlike most people, you can't take certain of her habits and use them to predict others. The same is true of her values and her inclinations. Just because she's an early riser doesn't mean she's never stayed up late into the night over a glass of wine, reminiscing about the past or dreaming of the future. She resists categorization at every point.

Perhaps, after all, that is the pinnacle of womanhood. Or just the truth of it. Nobody could ever fit her into a box.

Thus, such proto-typically "feminine" coloring was inaccurate, and in later years, it became obvious that these early paintings revealed much more of my own state of mind at that time than they did of their subject.

It seemed to follow that, until about the age of eighteen, it was rare that any subject emerged that I was not deeply familiar with. I painted my mother twenty-nine times over five years. My friend Rachiel, and her mother, who was a sort of second mother to me, appeared seventeen and twelve times, respectively. I had a few boyfriends that came up once or twice, but at this stage, I much preferred to paint women. Women were closer to me, but that did not necessarily mean that their shapes came easily. In fact, I found them to be much more challenging. They had a complexity that was not present in men, and that *need* not be present in men. My mother, for example, was always pink and gold, but her skin might emerge rippled or cracked or pregnant with water. She might be a child or a tangled and knobbed old woman, unrecognizable but for the deep arching back of her brow toward her eyelid, her slight lips. Men, on the other hand, were always overly vascular. If I began with a hand or an arm, I could usually recognize my male subjects right away, for men to me were still very primal, easily detected in complex figurations of veins.

So the catch always came later with women, and then the final devouring was faster, for once my subject was recognized, I could sense that something in my apprehension of her was always off, and thus the catch did not give me the satisfaction of possession—I had only captured some doppelganger that was created and then sloughed off for the subject's own protection. So, after the capture, I only wanted to finish and move on. With men, though, oversimplification didn't seem to be an error, or in cases where it was, I was less preoccupied by it. I have never quite yearned to understand men as I have yearned to understand non-men.

*

For a few months, I dreamt of younger versions of the old man from the deli. Our apartment was littered with stacks of books that seemed to reorganize themselves from

35

scene to scene. Herman Hesse was a frequent contributor, and I spotted Joyce and Melville more than once as well. We, or perhaps she and him, for I was never quite certain if the woman was me or if my only part in these dreams was that of a voyeur, but whatever the configuration, the pair never left the apartment.

In retrospect, the dreams were quite boring. They dragged monotonously, like a late-night talk show, so that a few mornings I awoke having spent the whole night watching her, perched reading like a twisted wire on a too-small wooden chair, only occasionally altering the position of her feet or arms. And all the while he would have just been flicking through sensationalist news reports and reruns of MASH.

Ultimately, the only thing of interest was the rats. They mirrored the man and Claudia/me in both action and speed. When Claudia or I read or cooked, rats sat on my or her shoulders peering into my or her book, or they scurried between the cupboard and the cutting board, rolling jars of spices or dragging vegetable scraps. And, in one dream, she or I made love to the young old man while pairings of rats mimicked us on the bedside table.

*

After having only painted the closest subjects of my life for eight years, at twenty-one I met a brooding teenager at a bus stop outside San Luis Obispo. He was spotty faced and deep in the throes of depression.

"I'm ready to die," he told me with the face of a stone.

"Would've done it a long time ago if it weren't for the fact that my girl's pregnant. That, and I don't want to give my sonofabitch father the satisfaction of coming home to find me limp and twirling by the light of the fireplace. It'd be like Christmas morning for the asshole."

I only nodded and tried to look sympathetic, occasionally offering up morsels of advice that were so cliché they caused my voice to drop an involuntary octave at their utterance. The kid and I both pretended not to notice.

"You're young," I woefully interjected during some lull in his story, "things are bound to get better with time…" and later, "Don't give up. Everything always works out in the end."

He nodded compliantly after both remarks, but didn't give them any response. When his stop came, he stood up.

"Thanks for listening to me I guess."

He departed without a backward glance.

Afterwards, the heat stayed in my cheeks for an hour or two. I knew I hadn't been any help. More to the point, though, I couldn't understand what had transfigured my image into a vehicle of reception for this kid. Why had he trusted me so unquestionably? There was nothing in our appearances that would have made us co-collaborators. I was older, probably five or six years so, and in plain dress— a black T-shirt and loose light-wash jeans. He had donned all black—skinny jeans, a long sleeved shirt, a hoody with the hood raised up (though we were in the desert in mid-July), and a ring on every finger. And he was pale, as though he hadn't seen the light of day in weeks. I, on the other hand, looked strong, and my skin was richly browned.

Maybe he'd just been on the brink in that moment, and he would've settled for anybody willing to greet him with a neutral smile, receive him in the adjacent seat without flinching away or turning to look out the window. But I wasn't convinced. Maybe, instead, it was that he thought he'd detected a kindred sadness in me, tucked so far beneath my belly, between a folded bus length of intestines, that even I was unaware of it.

I felt a flicker of rage. I resented the idea that a stranger might've thought he knew me better than I knew myself. I spent five minutes getting worked up into a frenzy, and then I got ahold of myself long enough to realize just how self-obsessed and uncompassionate I was being. I decided to just forget it. And within a day or two, I had.

The experience had been relatively insignificant. I don't mean to sound cold, but for me the kid was an archetype through and through. He was entirely familiar; someone I'd met a thousand times in high school. Moreover, I knew that, more likely than not, my cliché proclamations would later prove realities. He would be alright; he would not decide to kill himself.

I brushed away the memory and forgot him.

*

Dreams about Claudia and the old man became more and more sporadic until, at last, they ceased altogether. By then, the old man had appeared twice in paint. Claudia, though, significant as she once was for the realities of my subconscious, never showed her face. Instead, something altogether unheard of happened. Without warning or explanation, I lost the catch—the moment of recognition. For the first time in my life, I began painting people whose faces I could not recognize.

The first was a young man, aged about twenty. Two oversized ears poked through a bodiless mass of hair which hung limp about his shoulders. His mouth was soft, and his eyes sat back in graceful caverns like the eyes of my mother, so that you could imagine a drop of rain sliding down his forehead and dropping fast onto his upper cheek, avoiding the curve of his eyelid. A precipitous brow, like a fortress wall. In some moments, I felt I was on the verge of recognizing him. He was familiar, though perhaps familiarity had become a sensation inherent to my process. My subjects always seemed familiar until the moment they *were* familiar. With him, however, my paintbrush slid to a stop, and I knew that I was finished although I still did not know him.

I wracked my brain for weeks. I tried adding more detail to his thin arms, thinking that perhaps I'd prematurely taken the painting for finished, though this would have been unprecedented. I read through my book of dreams and tried to visualize the faces of obscure characters. I flipped through old photo albums and grade school yearbooks. Still, he did not emerge.

I began a new painting. This time, it was of an ancient woman, twisted, perhaps, from years of manual labor, but with strong features, like the wood of a wind-blown tree. She was dark as coal but flecked with blues and oranges that illuminated the scribbled tessellations of veins that gave shape to her hands and arms. With her, even the notion of familiarity evaporated. She was as much a stranger to me as the old man at the market had been.

And then it was only unknown face after unknown face. Strangers became the fabric of my every day. For five years, I produced theories about the appearance of my mysterious subjects and recycled them again and again, holding fast to one for six months and, when it grew too moth-eaten to let me sleep through the night, switching it out for an old one whose flaws I had tried to cover over with dust and mud. I grew intellectually distant from myself. Perhaps it seems strange, but without the catch, painting was only an extreme expenditure of energy without any satisfaction. Previously, every catch had been a small ecstasy. Painting had been like carving out a hollow in the shape of a particular person or moment and the catch had been a fastening of that person or image onto my heart. Now I spent my days carving my heart with holes whose shapes I couldn't apprehend, and at the finish, there was no object to be fastened.

*

There had been other moments when my methodology changed. Six months after I met the brooding boy on the bus, his was the first face to appear on canvas following the terminus of a debauched Clarise Lispektor series. Up to that point, I had only ever painted people whose influence on my life had been obvious—my mother, my friends, my favorite authors, a politician here and there. When their faces emerged in paint, there was a comfort in the fact that I knew not only who they were, but also, I understood more or less why they had appeared to me. But now, here was this inconsequential boy whose name I had forgotten ten seconds after he told it to me.

For me, this suggested an essential disconnect between my psyche and my conscious self. Previously, I had always thought of the two as working in conjunction—a well-oiled machine, if you will. But now, I realized that my psyche might be capable of taking pieces of mental information—memories, thoughts, experiences—and storing them until they festered between brain-folds where the synapses don't often snap. It was possible, then, that I might keep secrets hidden from myself. With the boy, the secret was obvious. I'd thought he'd been worth nothing to me, but in the end, at the very least, he'd been worth a canvas, an array of colors, and thirty-five plus hours of labor.

His appearance thus represented a betrayal. It meant, for me, that I was not yet capable of understanding myself.

Afterwards, the possibilities in terms of potential subject matter exploded. People with whom I had had only minor interactions began to appear in my work more and more frequently. I began to pay more attention to the world around me. Later, I would come to think of the interaction with the boy much differently. Out of a strange darkness, a night flower had bloomed. In the light of day, the minutiae of the world finally became consequential.

*

I got fired from my job at the market for "lack of engagement." My mind, it's true, had entered into a perpetual state of wandering.

I began working the janitor's night shift at a monolithic university. From eleven pm to seven am, I dusted bookshelves, wiped down tables and chairs, emptied trash-bags and scrubbed toilets in a library built to house twenty-thousand strong. It was a relief to be able to ease into my body during those shifts, to scrub away, with dust and ink-stains, the stress that had been gradually deposited in my spine and neck by impatient customers, hot-headed management, and the habit of speaking in a false voice. But seeing so few hours of daylight threw me even deeper into the haze of uncertainty. Painting and dreaming assembled in the daylight hours. They blurred into each other and turned light into an abstraction. Concrete reality, on the other hand, took the form of empty fluorescent hallways, Windex sliding over metal, and the smell of old books full of distant histories.

My mother tried to convince me to give up painting altogether.

"It's like any great love," she argued, "it is possible for something that was once incredibly nurturing to become, through the influence of time, toxic to the body and spirit. To separate from the object of love does not negate the beauty that once existed between you. It only proves that you are intelligent."

*

When I was six, my mother took me to the Metropolitan Museum of Art. She held my small freckled hand firmly in hers and led me about, making sure to read me the names fixed on tiny white squares to the right of each painting—Klimt, Renoir, Degas, Pollack, Kahlo. I believe she was attempting to show me that creation is a deeply individualistic act.

"Look here," she might have said, "this painting is full of energy and chaos. That is the recognizable mode of this artist. So then, can you guess, based on who we've already looked at, who might have made this?"

I hated this game. Then, I only found it confusing. But as I grew older and spent more time trying to understand art, I would always find exceptions to "the recognizable mode of the artist," and those exceptions made me question my original conceit of that mode until the whole thing splintered and I was forced to abandon it, left to feel that I would never understand even those artists that I loved the most.

It happened that on that day, we'd spent a lot of time on paintings from Picasso's blue period. Then, out of nowhere, we'd come across his portrait of Gertrude Stein.

I was transfixed. My eyes, breaking from their habit of flashing violently about, trying to take in everything at once, bore rigidly into Stein's canvased form. I could not be pulled away. I did not, however, find the painting to be beautiful. In fact, my fixation had nothing at all to do with the particular image before me. Instead, I was only wondering, in the deeply abstract manner that any six-year-old tends to wonder, how Picasso had managed to produce such an image. Had he simply sat in a room, Stein posed before him, and focused his thoughts and energy so intently upon her that she had become frozen in place? Was this truly her, stuck fast before me, caught in the threads of a canvas pulled so taught that she couldn't even twitch a finger, couldn't heave a tired sigh?

No, that couldn't be it. If the fate of the muse was to be caught eternally on a two dimensional plane, to be removed from the world of the living only to become a rendering, nobody would ever have revered the great painters as gods. Painters would only be cruel captors, muses only lost sufferers, and paintings would be banished to torture chambers and the fields where car-parts are kept by the thousands.

Being only six, though, I was not capable of organizing this flood of imagery into anything so coherent as a question—"how is a painting made?" Instead, I felt my mother's tugging hand once more, and, at last, I turned on my heel

and followed her to look at the work of the late impression-
ists, Monet and Pissaro.

*

Now, twenty-eight years later, I began to consider the
possibility that my earliest theory had been right after all.
That painting is an act of violence. After all, for all those
years, I had referred to a part of my own process as "the
catch," thus turning subjects into animals to be hunted and
gorged upon. Perhaps, I thought now, the past five years
had only been my subconscious attempting to reveal to me
the cruelty of my daily practices. Without the ability to feed
on my prey, I had made myself into the hunted. Five years
without a catch had made me weak. Soon, I knew, I was
headed for death if I couldn't bring myself to stop.

I decided, in January of my fifth year painting unknown
faces, to make one last portrait before I went in search of
another life. I could tell right away that it would be an old
man. His jawline was square, and the flesh of his neck and
lower cheeks was loose and malleable. He had oversized
ears, a long nose, and a very thin upper lip. Later, whatever
severity those features might have presented was brought to
equilibrium by the softness of his eyes. I worked on him for
three weeks, but it wasn't until I began to trace the metallic
line of his circular spectacles that I recognized him. It was
Herman Hesse, circa 1955.

Perhaps, I sometimes think, memory is only a random
constellation. A moment's perceived significance isn't, finally, at all corollary to its chance of being caught in memo-
randum.

*

I was deeply apprehensive. I had adored Herman Hesse in my late teens and early twenties, but he hadn't been seriously on my mind in years. His appearance was as illogical as the entirety of the last five years.

That night, during my shift at the library, I filled a bucket of soap and water too high and absently let it slosh over the bathroom floor. Then, traipsing a series of narrow hallways towards a storage closet where rags were kept, a sudden intuition led me to change direction. I made my way to a well-hidden stairwell of dusty concrete and descended to the third floor. I headed to the computer lab. Once I'd booted up a computer, I double clicked the search catalogue. "Hesse, Herman," I typed in at the top. Ninth floor, section P84. I took the stairs again and arrived slightly out of breath. There were close to one hundred books under Hesse. His entire collection, with seven or eight copies of each of the notables, and at least thirty volumes of theory and criticism. I picked out a copy of *Demian*, one of a few I recalled being quite fond of, but whose contents I had, fifteen years later, all but forgotten. It was an old copy, so I drew it to my nose and breathed in that deep mustiness that is as much a part of any book as the story within. Then I walked to a nearby table, pulled out a chair, and sat down, preparing to read. When I opened it, I saw that there was a note scribbled in ink on the inside cover.

*To Claudia,*
*with love*
*—1974*

There are thirty-four Claudia Rillings listed as New York City residents. I visited twenty-seven of them, rushing door to door, from Inwood to Coney Island, Harlem to Crown Heights, appalled with myself at every interval. For five years, it hadn't occurred to me. And now here it was. There had been a Hesse book in nearly every dream I'd ever had about me or her and the young old man. I found her on the twenty-eighth doorstep.

She was over seventy, and I just rounding the hump of thirty-five, but there was no mistaking it. She looked more like me than my mother ever had. In fact, the first thing I thought of when I saw her was an old film I once watched about cryogenic freezing. I imagined us as identical twins, her having been birthed naturally while I waited almost forty years to join her in the realm of the living. Standing before me now, her mouth had dropped slightly open and her eyebrows were raised at attention. I registered her shock as easily as if it were my own.

"Come in," she stammered, apparently not knowing what else to say.

Just to the right of the door hung a photo of her draped about the shoulders of a young man. She was aged about thirty. I could, quite literally, not find any dissimilarity between the subject of that photo and myself. Down to the faint suggestion of a dimple in the right cheek and the messy tapering of the eyebrows that left more than a few hairs individuated. I had stopped short, and she beside me, her gaze moving, almost with panic, between the faded photo and my face.

We stood like this, both of us looking back and forth between the photo and the other, for a long time. At last, social traditions required that we tear ourselves from this strange performance. I followed her to the living room. We sat in burgundy chairs lumped with age. Both of us crossed right leg over left and then wrapped right foot back behind left calf. For a few more moments, we watched each other, warily entranced. At last, she broke the spell.

"Who are you?" she asked abruptly, a hint of fear detectable in her inflection.

I paused for a protracted moment, trying to decide how to begin.

"Five years ago," I said at last, "I met a man in a grocery store. He gave me your name."

I paused for a moment. I was already having trouble explaining myself, so I decided to stand up. I figured I might be able to speak more clearly if I wasn't looking directly at her. I moved towards a cluster of photos on the mantel.

"Oh my god," I breathed.

"What," she asked pointedly, her fear and confusion threatened to combust into rage. "Look, you need to tell me exactly what's going on here," she continued, "I—"

"Claudia, please," I interrupted her, "Who is this?"

I gestured to the photo on the mantel. It's subject was a young man, aged about twenty. He had dark stringy hair that hung in strands around his shoulders, and his eyes were deeply set, like the eyes of my mother. His brow was overly pronounced. Precipitous even, like a fortress wall.

"Him?" she asked, more bewildered than ever, "that's my son, Lionel."

"Lionel Rilling," I whispered to myself.

"No, he's got his father's surname. Lionel Zavgren."

The name bore into me with an almost erotic satisfaction. It was a satisfaction that had been denied me so long that I felt energy virtually pour into my body at the name's sounding. Lionel Zavgren. It catalyzed an awakening. The quality of light in the room became more precise. The colors, which had been dull as corpses, saturated with life. Sounds sharpened, crackling and popping scrumptiously inside my ears. Recovering anorexics, I have read, sometimes experience a sensation akin to this one. With the reintroduction of food, the five senses grow stronger, and the sick body is often pleasurably surprised, not having registered the gradual weakening in the first place. I felt like a dying body coming back to life.

"Claudia," I said at last, my voice clear and firm, washed of its usual ridges by a certainty I hadn't felt in years, "I am a portrait painter. But for the last five years, since the moment I met that man, your old lover, in the deli, I have painted portraits of people unknown to me. Unknown because they have been the subjects, not of my life, but of yours."

*

Six months after I visited the MET with my mother, I was given a set of acrylic paints for my seventh birthday. At last, I discovered the secret that had alluded me when I'd stared down Gertrude Stein in shades of brown. That a painting was made from paint. That a painting was a fashioning of a still idea out of liquid color. That it was a manipulation of symbols—reds and blues, greens and browns—into a sign. Or perhaps not a sign, but a feeling, the distinct feeling of the artist in relation to the muse.

*

Claudia came back to my apartment with me that evening. I had to half-carry her up the four flights to my door, as she was quite a bit frailer that I had realized. It was an old railroad apartment, built in a straight line and crammed between a hundred likenesses. Only the front and back rooms—the kitchen and bathroom—had any windows, and since my bedroom was in the center, I used my bed as a table, having decided to sacrifice the traditional *kitchen* table in favor of a studio area with light.

"Would you like some water," I offered, stepping over the threshold behind her, but she had already spotted the paintings and was briskly making her way over to them in lieu of a reply.

About fifteen of them were clearly visible, and the rest were stacked against the walls in rows and columns, sometimes eight or ten paintings deep.

She moved silently around the room for a few minutes, and I watched her from the kitchen.

"Oh my god," she said at last, picking up a piece of loose canvas I'd been forced to, during a shortage of money and materials, remove from its frame in order to stretch another. Holding it up in the light, she suddenly burst out laughing.

"You know, this has got to be one of my fondest memories of us," she said, "Emily Mahdavi. What a riot girl."

She paused a moment, shaking her head and grinning like a child. Plunging into the liquid warmth of a former reality.

"We both went to this little art school up in the Hudson Valley. Nearby, there was a big public land reserve—Poets Walk Park, it was called. The place was huge; you could

49

walk for miles without seeing another soul. One day, in the beginning of our senior year I think it was, we'd been walking there for about an hour, and all of a sudden we came out of the woods onto this incredible, wide-open landscape. I swear, the land there was formed by its own intention. It narrowed and flattened as it approached the water, as though the original plan had been to shoot out, bridge like, strong over the great Hudson River. At the last moment, though, wits back about it, it had stopped short. It was daring and cerebral and full of grace. I hadn't known such places existed."

Still smiling, she moved absently towards my wooden painting stool. She sat down and draped the canvas across her lap. Then she curled into the image, head and neck bent over it, knees propping it up towards her face.

"So all of a sudden," she continued, "I get this overwhelming urge. I tear off all my clothes and start bounding down the hill and out onto the plateau towards the river. It's the golden hour—between five and six in early fall, when the world gets bathed in that primal orange precluding sunset and shadows dance under trees and bodies. Everything was just drenched in magic.

"So I'm darting like mad, trying to fill the illustrious moment with a bit of me, and meanwhile Emily's laughing her head off. She's got this old Nikon film camera with her and starts snapping photos of me. Then she steals my clothes and hides them up a tree."

Claudia and I were both in the early stages of fitful giggling now.

"Emily and I always played like that," she pressed on, "one of us would launch the other into hysterics with some ridiculous stunt, and then the laughing fiend could only be satisfied once she'd found some way to outdo the antics of the first."

She paused a moment, growing serious.

"Well, when the photos came back, they were really something. I was wild, through and through. My breasts were flying in every direction, the fat of my thighs quivered for the sheer length of my strides, my face was a swirl of heat, and my body hair curled with the milky sweet sweat of raw energy and adrenaline. This painting is the way her face looked as we sat together in my dorm room, examining the evidence. She was the only person I could ever have been that free with, and you could see that in the photos. I think it terrified her as much as it pleased her.

Anyway," she said, clearing her throat, "she died three years ago. Car accident."

"Sounds like she was really something," I said quietly, the warmth of a burgeoning fondness for my antique double swelling my cheeks full of blood.

"She really was," she said, more to herself than to me.

"You know," I offered, "I've got a few more paintings of her. She was one of the subjects that kept cropping up."

*

I spent the rest of that day weaving together my own image of Claudia via a series of winding anecdotes. For each painting, she'd ceremoniously announce the name of the subject, and I'd feel a rush of satisfaction, a little bit more life regained. Then she spoke of whatever memories cropped up. Soon, all the figures became connected, not only to the common point along all their intersecting axis— Claudia—but to one another. Many had friendships outside of Claudia or they were relatives or people connected by virtue of the fact that they had, at some point, brought Claudia substantial happiness in the form of a grilled cheese. It was, for me, an incredible relief to see that my mind, for five years, had been doing something more than plucking random images from the universe and laboring to record them. The chaos had found its origin.

Towards eleven in the evening, I drove Claudia from my home in Westchester back into the city. Her voice had gone hoarse from talking so much, so we listened to soft music most of the way, now quite at ease to sit quietly together as strange replicas, hurtling through space. When we arrived, she turned to me in earnest.

"Julia," she said, shwar-ing the 'J' so that my name sounded soft and round, "I'm dying."

"I —" I began in protest. "What?"

"Cancer. Stage four. It's been a few years coming."

I nodded and clenched my throat.

"I've only got a few weeks, you understand?"

I nodded again.

"I wonder if," she continued, "there's something you could help me do?"

"Of course. Anything," I whispered.

"The paintings you've made, of all the people of my life, I don't understand how it's possible. It isn't possible, I'm sure. But the strangest thing is, not only have you painted the people of my life, but you've somehow managed to paint them exactly as I've seen them."

"What do you mean," I asked.

"When you look at a photograph of someone," she said, "you often think, 'huh, that's so odd—they don't look like that at all.' But your paintings show something incredible. They show the people of my life refracted through me, as though I were the lens you peered through and used to focus each image. In some sense, what they show is not individual people, but people as they live—animated by their human connections."

I nodded softly in gratitude, letting my tears drip freely into my lap.

"I know that the paintings belong to you. They are five years of your life's work. But I wonder if there's any chance you might be willing to give them up, to help me spend my last few weeks delivering them. To all the people of my lifetime."

*

Four weeks later, only a few paintings—of people who were no longer living or who we'd been unable to track down—remained.

Emily's renderings were still propped against the south wall of my kitchen studio, and one afternoon, while looking again at the loose canvas that had prompted Claudia's first story, I noticed something strange. The colors in her hair had congealed, for lack of a better word. Strands that had been nuanced and complicated by strokes of blue and gold had all but lost their exceptional colors. Her hair sat flat as the fur on an unwashed dog, a two-dimensional mass of brown. At first, I assumed it was sun damage. But when I flipped anxiously through the other paintings I had left, they all seemed to have lost their vitality in some way or another. An ear without an ear canal, the lashes over an eye thinned and individuated. Perhaps, I concluded, caught up in all the magic of Claudia's stories, my paintings had taken

on a dynamic quality that had simply never been their reality. Maybe they'd always had these striking flaws.

I decided to look back at some older work, from before I
had started painting the people of Claudia's life. I pulled a
few of people I had never known well, thinking that they
would make the most astute comparisons; people I had seen
through the lens of particular moments, just as I had seen
Claudia's subjects through her. There was the toothless
fisherman I'd spoken with, beneath a bridge, at dawn.
There was a drunk man on a train with a bag full of beers
who'd wept to me about his young daughter, dead in a
house-fire. He'd wept so much that eventually he vomited
all over the train floor. And a woman with gum in her hair,
which I'd helped rub out with the peanut butter from a
sandwich I was carrying. We'd spent a heat-combustible
afternoon together, and she'd French braided my hair to
keep it from sticking to the back of my neck. There was,
too, the old man who'd scooted away from me with a look
of disgust when I boarded the subway dripping snot, tears
running so thick I was unable to see, throat clenched from a
heaving that eventually dispersed into shivers. He made me
feel lonelier than I ever had before.

There was no comparing these works with Claudia's
paintings, though. They were as good as anything else I'd
ever made. Claudia's, on the other hand, had somehow all
gone flat.

*

The funeral was six days later. It was strange to see all
my old subjects come to life. To see them embrace, recognizing one another after years of separation. To see the
ways their bodies moved, and how those who I'd painted as

54

young people had aged, their bodies twisting like man-groves. Many people asked me if I was Claudia's daughter.

"In more ways than one," was the only answer I could muster that felt true.

There were a few people that I'd met during the last few weeks. They lived close enough that Claudia and I had been able to deliver the paintings in person. One of them had been John, the old man I'd met in the deli more than five years before, the man who had inexplicably forged my con-nection with Claudia.

"You know, it's strange," he said to me, "I look at those two paintings you gave me all the time. But for the last few days, they've looked somehow different. The twitch has gone out of my lip and my cheeks have gone pale."

*

A few days later, I finished a new painting. It was so ob-vious. There she was with a tiny twitch in her lip, rosy cheeked, hair awash with complexity and nuance. There was meaning and significance in every stitch of canvas. Here, the flecks of light that had animated the painting we'd given to her old Italian professor, Karen Goodlad. There, a wrinkle along her jawline that recalled Hesse.

It was the image that exists at the end of every life, formed in bits and pieces by all the people who have given and taken, and who have been given to and taken from. It was the most beautiful painting I'd ever made; It was purely her.

# Junk
## by Christopher Fox

Another chunk of debris crashes into the cornfields be-hind my parents' house, burying itself in a mound of stalks and dirt. The impact rattles the plates on the table and the spoons in our coffee. Dad's wheelchair rolls back a few feet. My breakfast jumps into my stomach.

"I'll get the dishes," Mama says to me. "You get the shovel."

The first time this happened, Mama thought we were getting bombed. She heard the scream of hot metal through the air and dove under the table like she'd learned in the drills. Dad assumed the thud was Mama falling, and didn't bother to turn off the TV. I half-hoped it was aliens, coming to abduct me, but the Interior people said otherwise when they came around to collect the scraps.

We thought this was a one-in-a-million kind of thing, but we were wrong. Satellites crash so often now that 'rain-ing metal' should be a permanent fixture of our regional forecast—along with tornados, heat lightning, and drought. Like all those other things, we got used to it.

We keep the shovel by the back porch, next to the fire extinguisher and the wheelbarrow. Smoke rises up from the spot, and the air smells like a mix of popcorn and fireplace. I grab the shovel in one hand and the extinguisher in the other, and head toward the plume.

The crater is maybe ten feet across, the center deep as a grave. I have to fight for a few minutes to quell the flames, which spread along the edges and turn the snapped stalks brown, then black. I spray the embers with the extinguisher before burying them with the shovel, just to be sure. A couple stray flames wink atop nearby stalks like candles watching me work.

I sidestep into the hole to inspect the scene. Some sprigs of metal shine in the dirt, like the satellite's a seed that's begun to sprout. The debris is still hot, so working in the crater is a little like shoveling in a sauna. You sweat double. I pull most of the stray leaves and roots out of the way, flip some big rocks off the top and toss them over the crater's lip.

I'm just starting on the sides when I hear rustling in the stalks. I wonder if this visitor's wild or welcome. Turns out Mama's rolled Dad down the back ramp and pushed him through the crash site to survey the damage. His oxygen tank is tucked between what's left of his legs, and for a second I picture it blowing up.

"How's it going?" Mama asks. She has her hair up in a high bun, and still has on her apron from breakfast. It's beige with yellow flowers that blend in with the stains.

"Fine," I say.

"You need anything?"

"No, Mama, I'm fine."

"I swear if this keeps happening, we're going to have to move," Mama says. "It's like these things just keep giving up."

"Sounds familiar," my father snarls through his oxygen mask, watching me shovel and sweat.

"Would you like to try?" I ask, pointing the handle of the shovel in his direction, somewhere between his thighs and his chest. It's something he used to do to me when I was a kid and would interrupt his chores.

He laughs through a cough, or coughs up a laugh, and stares down the handle at me. Bits of dirt run slowly down the blade and bounce off my jeans.

"'Try' is an interesting word for somebody who doesn't have a job," he says.

I shove the blade back into the dirt, and stomp on it with my foot. Dust flies up into my face, and I push it out of my eyes.

When I look over my shoulder, Dad takes a big pull of air and without turning his head, talks to my mother. "I don't understand why we're even wasting our time on this one."

Mama gives me a look like she wants to say *He means the satellite.* But she doesn't say it. It's no secret that "this one" could mean me.

*

Mama rolls dad back inside, and I start chucking rocks with the shovel like it's a lacrosse stick. Occasionally some birds fly up, startled by yet another morning impact. Some part of me imagines getting one high enough it goes into

58

orbit, evens the score. But my meteorites don't have the escape velocity to leave.

Ever since the first few crashes, I've been reading about satellites, the sheer amount of junk we've put up there. Even before commercial space flight became a thing, there were hundreds of thousands of pieces of debris zooming around, ready to take a bite out of any passing craft. Now—between the number of missions, and the number of accidents—we're well over a million.

Somebody tried to model all the stuff we're tracking, the dangerous junk that's big enough to see. The picture looks like ants swarming a scoop of ice cream.

Now there's a law that says satellites of a certain age need to clean out their orbits and make their way back home before they add to the mess. Most of them crash into the ocean, and I imagine their plunking like skipping stones. But more often the valuable ones—the kinds Interior and Defense and private collectors come out to find—are directed towards certain "uninhabited" tracts of land. Apparently, our part of Iowa counts as uninhabited. Even the news channels have started calling us "fly-into" country.

I guess it's better than the alternative. I read about this thing called Kessler Syndrome. The idea is that when we've got so much stuff in space, some of it's going to collide; when things collide, they're going to break into a lot of pieces. More pieces means more stuff means more collisions means more pieces—until we've got a cloud of garbage circling the earth that grounds us for life. Somebody decided it was time to clean that shit up, because Lord knows we don't want to get stuck here.

Cleanup isn't easy. Even the smallest piece of space junk can ruin your vacation if it clips your window at 17,500 miles per hour, or punctures your suit when you're out on a walk. Not that it's better when it lands. I once saw pictures of a barn whose roof was taken out by a few inches of solar array. Even a single screw can do a lot of damage at terminal velocity.

I've spent weeks of my life fastening sheets of metal onto our roof. From above, our house must look like the hull of a capsized ship. Dad's the captain, ready to go down with it.

*

After a few hours my hands hurt from choking the shovel, and my palms burn hot like the sides of the craft. As I straighten up, I feel my shirt cling to my lower back. The sun surprises my eyes.

I walk around the side of the house so I can stretch my legs. Dad's been rolled in front of the TV, like always, the news turned up so he can hear it over his tank. The words that float out the window make the hairs on my neck bristle. *Terrorist. Liberal. Default. Coup.*

When I come into the kitchen, Mama's shucking corn for dinner. She rips them open quickly, revealing the rows of bright yellow kernels. The husks pile up next to the sink like green napkins. A few stray hairs stick to the front of her apron, like wispy spaghetti. I count the ears. There's probably a dozen more than we can eat.

"He doesn't mean it," she says. "We both want you here."

I can't help but snort a little, shake my head. I take water out of the refrigerator, and pour myself a drink. The glass feels cold on the pads of my fingers, and the liquid fills my chest with winter. A little goes down the wrong pipe—I'm drinking too fast—and I start to cough. I hear Dad coughing from the other room.

"He doesn't know what he wants," I say.

The TV blares a commercial for one of the junk rigs that roll down the interstate, mobile shops where you can sell your suborbital wares for cash. They're like storm chasers for satellites, connoisseurs of debris. I've got to have that satellite cleaned up by the time they pass through next. If the bills I've seen are any indication, we could really use the money.

"Do you know what you want, Sam?" There's a pleading quality to her voice, like a child asking for cake. She's been asking me that question ever since I've moved back, and six years later I still don't think I care.

*

When I get back to the crater, I assess the craft. Now that most of the dirt's been hauled away, the satellite looks mostly intact. It's big and boxy, like an oven, but should fit in the wheelbarrow just fine. How I'm going to lift it is another story.

I get started on the excavation. When you get a full sat like this one, you don't want to damage it. If the government or the company that owns it wants it back, they'll try to blame the nicks on the poor souls who found it. For a lot of the older stuff, the artifacts, law is if it lands on your property it's yours to sell. But the collectors are pickier than the government, docking dollars off the asking price for every "manmade" imperfection. You've got to know what you have is valuable, otherwise they'll talk you down.

I run back to the house to grab the firm bristled broom Mama uses to sweep the porch. I push the dirt off the top gently, like I'm a paleontologist with the weirdest dinosaur you ever saw. There's the rounded surface of a dish. A few antenna stick out like the remains of wings. A couple more rounds with the broom, and I see the ID panel. It reads *ECHO-V*.

*

It takes another hour to wrestle the ECHO onto its side, heave it into the wheelbarrow, and roll it back to the shed. The loose dirt shifts under my feet, and it's hard to get leverage. Reminds me of pushing Dad down the beach. The satellite is heavier than Dad, but just as grateful. I get it over the lip of the crater and the corn seems to part for us like the sea for Moses.

When I get to the shed, I look up "echo satellite" on my phone to see if it's valuable.

Turns out, the ECHO Program was launched after the cloud of space debris started interfering with satellite transmissions. Like the earlier programs named from myth, the NASA people thought they were clever. ECHO satellites were designed to amplify communication signals from Earth and act like relay stations to transmit through the clutter. *Enhancing Communications through Hazardous Orbits.* According to my phone, they launched nine.

Wikipedia claims that opponents argued the program only added to amount of stuff in space, that it avoided dealing with the actual problem. But isn't that what we've always done? Keep going rather than deal with the mess we've made?

Internet says the asking price for one of these is in the thousands, but there's a range. ECHO-I went for $60,000 at auction. But someone pawned off a fake ECHO-III a few years ago, and now the collectors are stingier than ever.

Either way, it'd be enough to help out or get out.

Dad rolls by the shed as I'm wiping down the ECHO, getting his exercise by doing a few laps around the house. I bet Mama needed a break.

I remember coming back the summer diabetes took his legs. The whole drive home from the hospital, he wouldn't stop criticizing my driving, my car, my haircut, my ex-girlfriend, my major. Pretty much every choice I ever made. Only time he shut up was when I when I had to lift him out of the back seat and put him in the chair. I don't think he ever felt so vulnerable as when his son held him like a baby, or when the feet he thought were there were not, and couldn't touch the ground. It took a few more minutes of that silence to realize the dampness near my shirt collar was tears.

He was both heavier and lighter than I imagined. I had to wrap my arms around him like a hug, the way I hugged the satellite to get it out of the dirt.

I sit and watch him for a minute, wheels spinning, arms pumping, sweat running down his forehead. The tank rattles a little bit, but he keeps going, gulping in air. He doesn't look in my direction.

When I came back a few years later, he looked at me and I couldn't tell if he was sad or angry, but every day since, we've gotten a little more of both.

*

Mama calls us in for dinner, which consists of the usual fare—corn, instant mashed potatoes, some mac and cheese, everything about the same color.

Dad rolls to the fridge to grab the ketchup, and when Mama sees him take it, she says, "Your blood sugar."

"It's a vegetable," he snaps. He grins as the red liquid spurts over his plate. Mama takes the salt and puts it on top of the fridge.

We normally eat in silence, or let my Dad try to tell us about the news. Today he seems like he's a different mood, and before we even say grace he says, "I think it's time you move out."

We've been here before. Since the day I moved back, he's been dropping hints, making suggestions. Last time the collectors came through and I was showing them what I thought was part of a 1960's space artifact (it wasn't), Dad was talking up the driver, asking how much he's paid and how I could get a job. That was a few months ago now, but it feels like he brings it up once a day.

"What is it this time," I say. "You hear somebody's hiring? Some new training program? Want me to call that truck driver?"

"I didn't pay for that degree just so you can shit around my house."

"Look who's talking," I say.

"Sam, stop," Mama starts.

"Why are you talking to me? Tell him to stop. He's the one who does nothing but sit around all day while I screw metal on the roof or put out fires or rebuild the fucking ramp. You guys shouldn't even be in this house, not while the sky is falling and *definitely* not while he's in that chair."

I look down at my potatoes. There's a clear puddle that shines where the butter used to be. I imagine pulling my fork through, like I'm aerating the soil in neat rows, and watching the butter flow down the canyons and escape onto the plate. I wait for Dad to make one of his usual cracks like, *maybe you should have studied drama*. I feel empty and full all at once.

"Get out," he says.

Mama tries to talk him down, but I don't. I push in my chair and go back out to the shed.

*

The only way to know if this ECHO is authentic is to open her up and find the serial number, and I've got nothing but time. There's a panel that, if the picture's right, used to be covered by a heat shield. Most of it's soldered together, but I find a four-by-six panel held in by recognizable screws.

I shake out the toolbox on the floor of the shed. Hammers knock the hardwood while the wrenches clank on top of each other. No screwdriver. I check by the tractor, look around the porch. It's getting dark, and I worry this will have to wait.

I come back into the house to look for a flashlight, or a screwdriver, whichever comes first. In the kitchen drawer there are receipts and stray buttons, rubber bands and prescription bottles. Crumpled near the back, I find several neon orange fliers. I pull out one that reads "Final Notice: Evacuate."

For a second I wonder how I could have missed this. How I could have missed the impacts getting bigger and more frequent, the visits fewer and more frequent. How everything changed and we pretended like it didn't.

I start yelling for Mama. Dad yells *Keep it down*, but the TV is so loud I yell back, *Turn off that crap*. Suddenly we're shouting about the news he watches and my education, rehashing every fight we ever had. Our own Kessler Syndrome in the living room.

Mama bounds downstairs, pounding each stair as she goes, like she's got to put out a fire. She's wrapped in her bathrobe, her hair still dripping wet. "Sam can stay," she yells. "We can be a family."

Her voice pierces all the noise. Then she looks at both of us, breathing heavy, before saying again, "We can go back to the way things used to be."

But we can't. I lift up the flyer dated a few months back. "Did you know about this?"

I can see the moment she realizes we're not just having the same old fight, that this one's bigger now, and her face goes white, then red. She starts weeping the way I did when I got caught in a lie—about a book report, or my grades at college—and felt like the world could end.

Dad wheels over to her and pats her on her lower back, offering whatever comfort he can without rolling over her toes. Without looking at me, he says, "You need to get out."

And all I can think is, *so do you.*

*

I never find the screwdriver. I never open up the satellite to see what's inside, peer into its dark cavity to understand what it has that lets it cut through space so easily, communicate so clearly.

Instead, I take a few pictures on my phone and send them to that collector dad made me talk to all those months ago. We schedule a pick up for early tomorrow, and they'll appraise it then. Either way, I don't know how else to help. Then I leave the shed, get into my car, and wonder if I should sleep or drive.

"Junk" originally appeared in *3Elements Review*.

# Mr. Chips and the Mango-Tango Mother Ship

by Alice Hatcher

Marylou was breaking it off with the human race once and for all, leaving the whole miserable lot for good, and this time for real. The whole thing had been a mistake from the start, an ill-conceived exploratory mission to gather data about evolutionary dead ends. High time had come to drive out to the desert, where she'd been deposited so many years ago—thirty-five, not that there was any point in counting, since no one had ever given a cold crap about her birthday or bothered to determine its exact date—to meet the Mother Ship and shake off the dust of this wreck of a planet. She'd already loaded her '96 Buick Century with her go-bag and a variety of human cultural artifacts (including the *Twilight* series in paperback and a collection of scratched CDs by the Go-Go's and Philip Glass), all the while nursing hopes that no well-meaning friend or distraught lover or stymied therapist would ever again tell her (because she'd heard it all before) that she was talking too fast, drinking and smoking too much, fucking too many strangers, driving too recklessly and laughing too loudly at the wrong time and basically, if you wanted to get to the heart of it, feeling too goddamn much when she wasn't feeling anything at all. Her brain hurt, really, when she even thought about it.

She'd left her so-called husband on the couch, watching a Super Bowl half-time performance by some kinky little biped in spandex tights. He'd had his head so far buried in televised tits that he hadn't noticed her going in and out of the house to load the car during the second quarter, taking breaks only to peek into the living room for an occasional glimpse of Aaron Rodgers, the only human being (certainly the only NFL quarterback) worth half a rat's turd, from what she could tell. The miserable specimen didn't even look up when she said she was going out to get some cigarettes. It served the son-of-a-bitch right to make his own damn supper, or at least reheat last night's leftover tuna casserole and then spend the rest of his allotted lifespan drinking beer with his knuckle-dragging buddies (nothing against apes, who seemed cognitively advanced, relative to humans, and until sexual maturity, quite congenial). Served him right to be shit-out-of-luck in the relationship department. The human race didn't need the likes of him reproducing, anyway.

She stood beside the Century with Mr. Chips dangling from her left hand by the scruff of his neck, mewling like nobody's business and scratching her bare thighs with his ragged claws. Mr. Chips sensed big things afoot, and he tended to be a skittish cat just anyway, probably from putting up with years of that no-account asshole's nerve-fraying ruckus—the endless noise of everything from Arizona Cardinals' games to Mad Men reruns to Metallica's *Death Magnetic* to X-rated video games that (he claimed) might get her in right mood if she'd just let go of the wrong one, whatever the hell that meant.

"We're just like Noah taking off in his ark, Mr. Chips," Marylou said, pushing the cat through an open window and into the Century. Mr. Chips peered over the edge of the seat, at a small fishbowl near the brake pedal. "I wanted to bring the best specimens home, sweetie, and only you and Lady Gaga made the cuts. No point overloading the car with two of everything from this ass-sucking clod of dirt."

Mr. Chips leapt onto the dashboard and pressed himself into the angled space beneath the windshield. Marylou studied his muddy paws and the tufts of black hair at the base of his ears, blew him a kiss and took a step away from the car to kick a patch of rust at the bottom of the driver's door.

"Only got one more trip ahead of us, you creaky piece of junk. Just got to get us beyond Gates Pass. Don't let me down, now." She slid into the driver's seat and placed her feet on either side of the fishbowl. "Don't you worry, Lady Gaga. I got it all under control. In an hour or so, we're leaving this shit-can of a car in the desert and heading to Q System."

Marylou turned the ignition key, listened to the engine struggle to life, and reached between her legs to tap the side of Lady Gaga's bowl.

"You'll be perking up once the Mother Ship gets escape velocity. Q System's just north of the Big Dipper, and if you want, we'll stop on our way home and let you take a swim in it. It's one big floating fish bowl in outer space, Lady Gaga. You're gonna have stars and planets to swim around instead of your dumb castle, Mr. Chips is gonna get some cosmic catnip, and we're all gonna be happy for a change."

Marylou trailed off and began shaking. She'd known for years (even if she'd been scared to admit it for too damn long) that the gig was up. Over the past few weeks, she'd been happy (too happy, her therapist would have said if

Marylou had kept her last appointment) and relieved to have finally made the difficult decision to end her mission on Earth, but now exhaustion was clouding her thoughts and muting the elation she'd felt a half hour before, when she'd pulled her go-bag from the bedroom closet. She sat quietly for a moment, studying a portion of the dashboard melted weeks before by an ashtray fire. Beneath a ridge of blackened plastic, the check engine light glowed faintly.

The light had come on three months ago, the same day a burst of static interrupted an infomercial about a fat-burning vacuum cleaner and floated from the TV screen, assumed the shape of a snake and slithered into her brain. In terror, she'd sampled channels in rapid succession, trying to exorcise a steady hiss from her mind, and finally found refuge in the sight of Ellen DeGeneres interviewing Aaron Rodgers. She'd stood transfixed by Ellen's gleaming white teeth and ruminating on her own unshakeable sense of estrangement until, in an inhuman act of mercy, Aaron Rodgers had dissolved into soft static, convinced her to *r-e-l-a-x* and whispered what she'd long suspected—that she was an alien stranded on Earth, a hyper-advanced being planted on a desolate rock to gather data about barely sentient bipeds. She'd turned the rabbit ears one way and another, measuring each oscillation of static until she knew without a doubt that she'd been born for a better life in a better body stroked by a better mate, and that her eyes were meant to behold velvety green skies illuminated by pumpkin-shaped moons.

For weeks, she'd taken long drives and trolled the radio waves for messages from the Mother Ship—each embedded in larger strings of information about Iraq and Mick Jagger, and on one occasion, two kangaroos that had escaped from a suburban backyard—and identified algorithms for confirming the content of each encoded transmission. She learned that the Mother Ship had delivered her in the shape of a human baby to the Saguaro National Forest; and that hours later, a middle-aged man who'd pulled off the road to take a leak had discovered her and (alarmed by her blistered stem-cell skin) dropped her off at a fire department. She heard, too, the soft blips of the Mother Ship returning to collect and carry her, exhausted, back to Q System—the soothing voice of a long-lost parent calling her home. Now that she was out of the house and away from her primary human subject, she could talk freely with Mr. Chips.

"She told me to abort the mission and come home, Mr. Chips. We've learned all we're gonna learn about the human race. She told me to signal them when we get to that pull-off beyond Gates Pass. Supposed to turn the radio to the far end of the dial and let it sit for awhile and then go back and forth until they hear us."

She looked, one last time, at the ranch house she'd foolishly called home for five years and felt a twinge of shame. To have failed at such a simple mission seemed a disgrace. She hadn't learned a damn thing about human relationships except that they were nothing but institutionalized exercises in misery of the most eviscerating kind. The simple fact was that she'd never managed to blend in with humans in just about any kind of situation, and her unremitting alienation had exhausted her. Twice since seeing Aaron Rodgers on the *Ellen Degeneres Show*, she'd even turned her back on the Mother Ship and denied her extraterrestrial origins, despite overwhelming evidence that she didn't (and couldn't possibly) belong to the human race: the absent birth certificate, the invariably failed stints with successive foster families, repeated expulsions from even the worst of Arizona's schools, her checkered employment history, drunken outbursts at weddings, and her indifference to things most others seemed to hold dear, from baptisms to baby showers to church raffles to mint chocolate Girl Scout cookies.

She listened to an ad for teeth-whitening gum and lit a cigarette. "Can't say I didn't try. Well, what happened on Earth stays on Earth. Just like Vegas, Mr. Chips. Time to scrape the shit from the bottom of our shoes, or I guess your paws. We're going to a much better place."

She rolled back into the street and turned the radio up loud. Mr. Chips folded back his ears and pressed against the windshield. She braked for a moment, stroked Mr. Chips and pushed the gas pedal to the floor. The car shuddered, bucked, backfired, nearly expired and then lurched around a corner. When the car settled into third gear, she blew a stream of cigarette smoke through her open window and began fishing cans of cat food from the go-bag.

"See, I thought of you, Mr. Chips," she said, holding up a 39-cent can of chicken liver fiesta. "Might take you some time to get used to the chow in Q System, but you'll have something to tide you over. Don't you worry about me, Mr. Chips. I brought some of my own provisions to ease the transition back home."

She slid a bottle of Popov from the go-bag, braced it between her scratched thighs and untwisted its cap. Mr. Chips sneezed and recoiled; Marylou cursed as the cap slipped from her grasp and fell into the fishbowl. She rested the fingers holding her cigarette on top of the steering wheel and reached down between her legs.

"Guess you wouldn't like vodka in your bowl," she said, pulling the cap from a fan of plastic coral. "Shame the stuff don't agree with fish, because you're missing out, Lady Gaga. Vodka's about the only thing worth taking back to Q System."

Marylou tossed the cap onto the street before a strip mall fronted by Food City, Factory 2-U, Family Dollar and an Eegee's advertizing Mango Tango slushies on its scuffed marquee. She pulled a Glock from the go-bag and pointed it out the window. "Fuck you twice, Food City. This time you're gonna feel the door on *your* ass on my way out." She laughed and drew the gun back into the car, untangled her fingers from its trigger guard and slid it under the passenger seat. Mr. Chips crept to the edge of the dashboard and peered intently at Marylou. "Don't you worry, Mr. Chips. I'm not crazy enough to get us arrested when we're so close to getting the hell out of here."

Past Westside Liquors, the lights of Tucson faded and the road began to rise. Marylou lifted the bottle of Popov to her lips, tilted her head back and then wedged the bottle between her thighs.

"You know he gave that gun more attention than he ever paid me." She massaged the tips of Mr. Chips' ears. "Oiling it up and talking to it like it was his girlfriend. Probably jizzin' himself the whole time. Wait until the folks back home see the jerk-off's little cap gun. He might not miss me, but he's gonna cry like a baby when he finds that thing gone. Screw these humans six ways from Sunday if they're all committed to killing themselves."

Past the Desert Life Taxidermy Museum, the steering wheel vibrated and the engine whined and Marylou pressed the gas pedal to the floor to sustain a sense of lift at the top of a small incline. For a moment, the radio's static slipped from her mind and she was alone with Mr. Chips, floating weightless over a dark valley. She felt the pleasant pull of gravity in her lower abdomen as the car descended into a gentle curve. The road straightened out, and her headlights spilled across a pale snake stretched across the road. Marylou pressed her flip flops against the brake pedal and her back against the seat; Mr. Chips extended his claws and dug into the dashboard; Lady Gaga angled her pelvic fins to counter the force of water sloshing over the side of her bowl; the Century skidded slightly onto the shoulder and came to a halt. When a cloud of dust dissipated, Marylou watched a rattlesnake inch across the road.

"That moron I called my husband would probably kill it, even though it isn't hurting anyone. Just rattling along and minding its own business. Only difference between that snake and the man we just left is two feet and ten toes, and on the other side of the equation, the brain in that snake's little head."

Marylou extinguished her cigarette in the gum wrappers filling her ashtray, lit another cigarette, and when the snake's tail disappeared into the roadside scrub, started towards Gates Pass, thinking the stars were closer than they'd ever been, and that if she touched the sky, she might feel something like satin. At a rise in the road, she looked down into the dark valley beyond Tucson.

"Down there is where we're meeting the Mother Ship. Where they left me. Why they let me grow up in this place is beyond me, but everything will be explained to us on board. The Mother Ship moves in mysterious ways, Mr. Chips. Maybe I was supposed to save you from this trash heap, because this is no place for a cat to grow up. No country for old cats. They ought to make a movie about that."

She rested her cigarette on a strip of melted plastic edging the ashtray and reached up beneath her shirt. "What kind of species has such uncomfortable breasts? Evolutionary advantages, my ass." She twisted her shoulders and slid a lacy red bra through her shirtsleeve. "Won't be needing this where we're going," she said, throwing the bra onto the road. "I gotta say, this body has been a load of bullshit, between cramps and cravings. Sex is the only good part, but even that leads to all sorts of problems no one's got time for. You could spend your whole life in a doctor's office, getting shots and IUD's put in and having people want to tie your tubes, saying it's for your own good. It would be the vet's for you, so be glad they stole your nuts at the pound before you had time to think about it."

She took several small bottles from her go-bag. "Might as well ditch the meds while we're cleaning house, Mr. Chips. These humans have a diagnosis for everything that's any fun. Having sex. Drinking. Smoking. Staying up late." She pulled her cigarette from the edge of the ashtray and pressed it into the corner of her mouth. "Thought I'd bring some samples of these goddamn pills back to the Mother Ship, but there's no point in killing a good buzz in Q System." She tossed the bottles onto the road, glanced once at the rear-view mirror and descended into the valley. "Damn meds took the life out of everything, including the old vajayjay, but maybe we can blame the ex-husband for that."

When the road leveled, she coasted onto a small gravel pull-off and killed the engine, leaving the radio tuned to static on the far right end of the dial. She contemplated a swathe of stars at the edge of the Milky Way and listened to coyotes yipping in the distance. After a moment, she took a swig of Popov and drew a pouch of catnip from the go-bag.

"Have your last pinch, Mr. Chips. Trust me, baby, you're not gonna need this stuff to feel good where we're going. The Mother Ship connection's gonna hook you up with something sweet. And you'll be the only cat in the galaxy. Everyone's gonna buy you fancy collars and all sorts of toys and drive you around the solar system in a winged limousine."

Mr. Chips slid his front paws down the glove compartment and lowered himself onto the passenger seat to root around in a small pile of dried leaves and stems. After a moment, he began kneading the seat cushions and chewing on the frayed hems of Marylou's denim shorts. Marylou hummed along to static and studied the sky.

Several minutes passed before hard white light filled the rearview mirror. Marylou gripped her Popov bottle and leaned forward. "This is it, Mr. Chips. I'm going home. This is the end of those cum-guzzling hypocrites in Food City calling me white trash and charging too much for cat food made out of horse guts. It's only the best for us, after this."

As she finished speaking, a car rounded a bend in the road and passed the pull-off. Marylou leaned back in her seat and stroked Mr. Chips between his shoulder blades until he collapsed beside her thigh. "Thought it was the Mother Ship." She lifted Lady Gaga's bowl from the floor and placed it beside Mr. Chips. "It won't be long," she said. "I want us all to be ready."

Four hours later, Mr. Chips crawled into the foot well in front of the passenger seat and started pawing the carpet. Marylou tugged a strand of hair falling loose from her ponytail.

"Whole damn desert's one big litter box, but I can't let you out, Mr. Chips. Too many things out there like to eat cats. All kinds of snakes, the two-legged and no-legged kind, and coyotes and javelinas who'd snap you up for a snack. You hang in there, Mr. Chips, because we'll be leaving soon. On the Mother Ship, they got litter boxes filled with diamonds and rubies. You'll be shitting shrimp and pissing pure cream."

When dome light began to dim, Marylou scanned the dial and listened to bits of news about football scores and wars in far away places, a celebrity psychiatrist analyzing a sex scandal involving three politicians and a pro tennis player, and Bruce Springsteen singing about the Magic Rat driving his sleek machine and a girl sitting on the hood of a Dodge and the two of them taking a stab at romance. Two military transports passed overhead, and she decided that air traffic was making it hard for the Mother Ship to detect her signals, faint static transmissions now buried in broadcast chatter. She looked at the vodka left in her bottle, the slow rise and fall of Mr. Chips' chest, the flecks of catnip floating in the fish bowl, and Lady Gaga turning in slow circles around a tiny castle.

"If the Mother Ship isn't coming for us, Mr. Chips. I'm sure as hell not going back to the way we lived. Maybe you and Lady Gaga and me ought to chuck it all in. Cash our chips at this crazy casino. Never figured out how to get along with anyone, and there's no two ways around the fact this mission failed. Wasn't more than a few minutes of it that made any sense, and I don't think there's any hope of figuring the shit out at this point."

She slid the gun from beneath the seat and cradled it in her lap. "In the hospital, some of the ladies used to say having babies gave meaning to life. Fact is, Mr. Chips, I didn't want a baby. Wouldn't know what to do with one. Don't even know what kind of parts I have inside of me. Alien parts, maybe." She trailed her fingers along Mr. Chips' hind legs. He stretched his back, splayed his paws and curled back into himself. "I can hardly think straight enough to take care of you and Lady Gaga half the time, between the football blaring and the shit-bag neighbors mowing their grass and leaf blowing and raising hell in their pool. Forget a howling baby. There's no place for one more in this world."

She held the gun to Mr. Chips' head, stroking him behind the ears with one hand and trailing the muzzle beneath his chin with the other. She'd kill Lady Gaga right in her bowl, even if it caused a big mess. Dumping her onto the gravel beside the car and letting her flop around while she drowned in the Earth's shit-awful atmosphere would be cruel. It would be the human thing to do. As for herself, she'd pop herself the same way she popped Mr. Chips, sending one bullet straight through the static and into the center of her brain.

"The Mother Ship doesn't care about us," she whispered. She lifted the gun to her lips to feel the touch of cool metal on her skin. "It'll be quick, Mr. Chips. Death. That's one thing that comes quick, at least quicker than anything else, from what I can tell from all that shit on TV."

She lowered the gun, and with her finger still curled around its trigger, scanned the radio dial until she found Bruce Springsteen's voice again. Mr. Chips rose on his two front legs and yawned.

Marylou felt around on the seat until she found her lighter. "It would've been nice to think there was at least one of them, one person that would have been nice to you. I think Bruce Springsteen would have understood us, Mr. Chips, but who the hell really knows, since we never met the guy. He just makes sense more than most of them."

She hummed along with Bruce Springsteen, now singing about parking lot visionaries and backstreet girls listening to records and two hearts beating through a night so tender, and she remembered downing shots and popping pills and fucking in the back seats of countless rusted cars, each with the same failing brakes and the same damn check engine light on their dashboards, feeling alive and defiant for at least a few fleeting instants before sadness flooded everything and some stranger's sweat dried on her skin; driving as fast as she could around mountain bends because, everyone said, she was around the bend just anyway; singing as loud as she could while the wind whipped through her hair; tripping and falling without feeling any pain until someone pointed to the blood seeping from some new wound; laughing it all away and listening to loud music to drown out the sound of jets tearing apart the sky and leaving vapor trails across the face of the moon.

"Screw it, Mr. Chips. We're not going out like this. That song wasn't long enough, and we're going to have to wait and listen until we hear it again, and anyway, it isn't right to check out without having ourselves one last fling. Having a decent drink instead of sucking piss straight out of this bottle." She sprinkled some catnip onto the passenger seat, placed Lady Gaga back on the floor and turned the ignition key. "Mr. Chips, I just can't leave this shithole without having proper sex one last time, a roll in the proverbial hay with someone other than that jackass on the couch, if only so this mission won't be a complete waste. It's only right, and if that don't matter, it's what Mr. Springsteen would want us to do."

It was nearly midnight when she parked in a corner of Eegee's parking lot and propped a heavily laced Mango Tango slushie on her knee.

"Best delivery system for vodka I ever found, in case you're wondering Mr. Chips. Humans don't know much, but they know how to get messed-up pretty good, so I guess I did learn something from all of them."

She sat with her elbow on the door, humming to the memory of Bruce Springsteen's Jungleland and looking up at the sky, imagining the Mother Ship moving above the dome of haze obscuring the stars. Mr. Chips sat in the passenger seat, nibbling the edge of a hamburger patty. Lady Gaga, elevated to the dashboard, hung above her castle, fanning the water with her gills and fins to maintain her suspended state. Marylou was studying the streetlight passing between the spines of Lady Gaga's translucent fins when a rusted red pickup backed into a nearby space. She lit a cigarette and watched a sinewy young man in oil-stained jeans step down from the truck's cab. When he turned around, she didn't turn away.

"Say, can I bum a smoke from you? I can give you a quarter, if that's cool," he said.

She imagined the color of his eyes and the feel of his hands smoothing over the scratches on her thighs. She waved away a quarter and started fishing around in her purse.

"They're just Pall Malls. Trying not to spend all my money on the things."

"No need to apologize. I don't got any, so I ain't got nothing on you." He brushed Marylou's fingers as he accepted her cigarette. He took a few steps away from the car and turned back around.

"Sorry to keep bothering you, but you got a light?" She held out her lighter, and he bent down and eyed Mr. Chips and Lady Gaga. "Got a pet store on wheels."

"That's Lady Gaga. And that's Mr. Chips. He's not really a pet. He's more than that."

"I get you. I used to have a dog named Jordie. Died last year. I think about him every day." The man blew a line of smoke into the air and drummed his fingertips softly on the roof of the Century. "Cared about him more than I care about most people. Life is strange that way."

"Mr. Chips and I are in it together," Marylou said. "Wherever we are. To the end."

Mr. Chips leapt on the dashboard, and the man rubbed his thumb and fingertips together to draw his attention.

"He isn't gonna take off if he comes near the window, is he?"

"He'd never run off on me."

"Smart little guy." The man leaned through the open window and rubbed Mr. Chips behind the ears. "How's that

Mango Tango? Maybe it's none of my business, but I was wondering if maybe you were out partying."

"You a cop or something?"

"I ain't no cop."

"Then maybe I have been."

"You ain't the only one. You have fun tonight?"

"Not so much. I didn't get to a party on time. There was no one there when I showed up."

"Doesn't sound like it was much of a party to begin with."

She shrugged. "Mr. Chips likes you." She leaned forward to brush her lips against Mr. Chips' whiskers. "He might be right about the party, baby," she whispered into a tuft of soft fur.

"You always take him to parties?"

"Didn't want to leave him alone tonight." She leaned back in her seat and watched the man's index finger moving back and forth along Mr. Chip's upturned chin. "Just moved out of my place, and there's no way I was leaving him behind."

For a moment, they pet Mr. Chips in silence and smoked. For a moment, Marylou felt at peace.

"If you and Mr. Chips aren't going anywhere right now, I can get myself some Mango Tango. We could just chill a bit. If you smoke, I got some weed."

"Mr. Chips has some weed, too." She stroked Mr. Chips' tail. "Hydroponic organic catnip. Actually, it's just regular catnip. Can't afford the good stuff, but we will someday."

The man ground his cigarette on the pavement. "You or Mr. Chips or Lady Gaga need anything?"

She shook her head and watched him walk into the hard orange and yellow light filling the space between Eegee's entrance and scuffed marquee. Marylou looked up towards the sky and imagined strange constellations and floating pumpkins and the Mother Ship hovering above, watching her every move and placing, in her path, all she needed to make the duration of her mission more tolerable; she imagined that she'd just experienced something some humans liked to call grace.

"He seems pretty decent for a human, and he's sure as shit better looking than the last one. Maybe we still got some work left to do here before the Mother Ship comes, and it is going to come, because she didn't forget about us. I can feel it, Mr. Chips."

She stroked the side of Mr. Chips' face and felt the presence of the Mother Ship moving across a plain black sky, static electricity between her thighs and a hint of moisture in the night air; she felt a strange hope that the man wouldn't tell her, at least right away, that she was talking too fast or drinking and smoking too much or laughing too loudly at the wrong time or, if you wanted to get right to the pounding heart of it all, feeling too goddamn much for any one person stranded on a dying planet.

"Mr. Chips and the Mango-Tango Mother Ship" originally appeared in *34th Parallel Magazine*.

# Good Times

by Alexander Jones

Art shackled his bicycle to the chain link fence off the pedestrian path in the park and sat down on the bench next to Ray. Ray, slouched against the thick wooden slats, took a hand out from the pouch pocket on his hooded sweatshirt and the two lightly touched knuckles.

"What's doing?"

Art shrugged, adjusting himself on the cold wood. "You know. Same shit."

Ray nodded. "I know."

They both stared across the path at the dirty river and the twinkling lights of the city on the far shore. They listened to the muted traffic sounds of horns blaring and engines revving from the highway overpass in the sky above them. Car exhaust drifted and settled to the ground, the smell less burnt and acrid at this distance. Layered beneath was the sweet autumn odor of rotting leaves, signaling the impending winter.

Farther down the path, an old man with pock marks on his face cast a line into the gray water. Otherwise, they had the park to themselves.

"What's he gonna catch, fishing this river?" Art asked.

"Cancer." This joke never got old.

Art slapped Ray's thigh and rubbed his hands together. "So. Whatcha got?"

Ray grinned. "You're feeling it? You want it?" Then, with a slight teasing edge to his voice, "You need it?"

"Yeah, I want something. It's cold out. Something to lift the blues."

"But do you *need* it?"

"Stop busting my balls." But he had no animosity, no annoyance. Just another part of their little ritual dance.

Ray shrugged. "Alright." He wagged a finger, "You know, you do too much of this shit and you won't remember—"

"And I won't remember who I really am anymore," Art singsonged. "Right."

Cracking his knuckles, Ray reached under his sweatshirt and came up with a worn brown leather satchel about the size of a hard cover book. He slowly unzipped and flipped it open.

Ray called it his twonky. He'd named it after a science fiction story, he had once explained.

On one side, snuggly tucked into little pockets were vials of various sizes filled with a rainbow of colored gasses. Some labeled, some not. All firmly stoppered. On the other side were different sized empty vials and ampules, a pipette, a baggie of spare stoppers, some notes scrawled on scraps of paper.

Ray pawed through the collection of colored vials, pausing at a yellow one. "A kid, playing with a Labrador puppy."

"You serious? That's a commercial for laundry detergent or something."

Ray smiled. "You like to bike. How 'bout a cyclist in an important race? Bought it a week ago. Tour duh France. Last few miles, exhausted, wanting that trophy so bad. Exhilarating. Inspirational shit. You can feel the wind in your hair."

"I feel the wind in my hair right now," Art answered, a smoggy breeze wafting down from a tractor trailer overhead. "Besides, that sounds like it's been used a few times already. Third, fourth generation. Right?"

Ray lit a cigarette. "Now who's busting balls?" He smoked. "But you're right, it's been passed around a few times, but it's still pretty clear. Have I ever steered you wrong?"

"We're cool."

Ray tossed his cigarette. "I've got something special. A girl."

"A girl?"

"A woman." Ray nodded his head. "Not just fucking her. An entire relationship with a beautiful woman. Storybook romance. I got it from one of the washouts down at the university. Not some blowup doll fantasy, either. A real relationship."

Art licked his lips. "Is it fresh? No thin spots, no hiccups? How much?"

"It's been a while, you know? I'm reluctant to part with her."

"I thought you were a terror junkie. You getting soft?"

"A hundred."

"I haven't got a hundred."

"There's an ATM at the bodega."

"I don't have a hundred. Besides, remember that guy tortured by the Chinese secret police? I gave that to you for practically nothing."

"Yeah." Wistful, he said: "That was something. Only thing better was what I got from that Holocaust survivor in my mother's apartment building." He tittered. "Good times."

Art didn't want to hear about that again. "So you owe me."

"True. But I'm not letting go of her for just money alone. On principal. Nothing scary ever happened to you?"

"I OD'ed once."

"Coke or Heroin?"

Art smiled at him. "Speedball. Best of both worlds, right?"

Ray shook his head. "Not for me."

Art looked over at the river, at the ripples extending from a bridge pylon in the center, lapping against the stone barrier at the edge of the park. The gray brown water held a shifting reflection of the city's lights. A protracted blast from a car horn came from the bridge.

Ray touched his shoulder, and when Art turned, gave him a glass vial. About three quarters full, it held a coppery red smoke. Art shook it and the smoke languidly responded to the motion. "Dense."

"Yeah, it's a whole relationship, like I told you."

"It's red," Art said, the heavy smoke drifting as he shook the vial again.

"Hey, red's the color of passion, am I right?"

Returning the vial, Art said, "So what, then?"

"Fifty. And something horrible."

Art dug through his pockets and handed Ray a wad of money. Then, touching his chin, he leaned his head back against the cold wood of the bench, eyes closed. The dread of coming home from school, walking around the block a couple extra times, waiting for his father because his father used to beat him with a doubled over belt. Getting caught with the belt buckle a few times. He'd pissed himself once, and pissed blood after the beating he caught for pissing himself in the first place. As a teenager, he'd broken into a junkyard to find a quiet place to get high, but a Rottweiler started chasing him. He remembered that clearly.

Opening his eyes, looking out at the water, Art thought of it. His best terror. Better than the mangy dog, or the belt.

"You got something?"

Art nodded. "It's good."

"It better be. You only gave me 43 dollars."

"It's a fair trade."

Ray held up the vial. Sunlight caught and projected the smoky red color onto his washed out sweatshirt. They both stared at it and Ray danced the vial around, the reflected red light shifting around on his shirt. "Want to take a sample?"

Art shook his head. "Have you ever steered me wrong?"

Ray produced an empty vial from the twonky.

"Smaller."

Ray handed him another empty vial, half the size of the one holding the relationship.

Art rubbed his eyes and stared at the churning river water, remembering everything, fastening on to details, his emotions, his beating heart, playing it over in his head and over again, over and over, faster and faster. When the memory started to spin, Art took it into the palm of his hand. He gently rolled it into a ball and squeezed it, compressed it to the size of a dinner roll and then smaller to the size of a golf ball, then smaller still to the size of a vitamin pill, careful not to lose anything, careful not to fracture it or fold it too many times, careful not to melt it with his body heat, and when he had the memory just right, he placed it right on the end of his tongue and drew in a deep, diaphragmatic breath.

Uncapping the vial he exhaled sharply through his mouth and the memory flowed into the tube. Art swiftly covered the opening with his thumb and then pushed in the rubber stopper.

The color inside the clear glass was the same color as the river water.

"That was good. You're getting to be a pro."

"I found a book about yoga and meditating. Expand your mind, control your center. Shit like that."

Ray handed him the red vial. "Maybe you'll get tantric with the girl."

"Maybe."

Overhead, rush hour traffic crawled. The old man had caught two fish, flopping around in a sack at his feet, and was loading up the line again. They watched as he cast.

"You wanna do them together, or wait till you get home?"

Art shrugged. "Whatever."

"Let's do 'em here."

"Sure."

They touched their vials together, toasting.

"To pleasant memories."

"Good times."

Ray popped out the stopper, held the vial to his nose and sniffed all of it in a single shot. Art opened his and savored the smoke.

*The campus gallery doesn't open for another hour, but there are already people inside. They're standing around and talking, pointing and gesturing at things, smiling or maybe trying to appear erudite as they hold forth on this or that. The gallery strikes the right blend of open space and bright lighting without being harsh or sterile. Those lights are extra soft fluorescents, I know because I'd installed them a week ago, nervous at the top of a twelve foot ladder.*

*In some places the floor is polished wood, in others it's a sepia toned carpet which I'd vacuumed and steamed earlier in the day. I smile, the way I usually do when I get assigned to work in this area of the school. The paintings are someone's work, displayed in the gallery, and the gallery display is my work. I stick around for the exhibits; a part time chemistry undergrad doesn't get enough exposure to the artistic types. I'm deliberately adding to my well-rounded education, learning things I wouldn't learn without the effort. Making myself cultured. Plus my boss thinks I'm clean cut enough to represent the maintenance department.*

*There's a girl standing alone, off to the side, close to one of the walls, staring at one of the smaller paintings. I remem-*

ber first being aware of her hair, a deep red flowing over the collar of her shirt. Irish? I wondered.

"You like it?" I ask, walking up beside her.

She shrugs. "You?"

I look at the painting, thinking of something to say, something on point and witty to make me sound smart, something to impress her with my depth of artistic insight and rapport, because I already know that it's her own painting. No one in this gallery stands in front of one painting, staring, unless it's their own.

I come up short on the sagacious artist front, so I step in a little closer, squinting theatrically. "It's cocked."

"What?" she asks, forehead wrinkling, drawing up her little button nose.

I grin at her when our eyes meet. "I said that it's cocked." I continue. "Cocked. You know…"

When her expression shifts to puzzlement, my grin widens. "Tilted." I hold my forearm at an incline.

"Oh." Her face relaxes as a thin smile comes to her lips.

"Oh?" I repeat. I want this girl to smile, really smile at me, and maybe laugh, or I want to know that I tried even if I failed miserably, so I say, "Oh , did you think I was saying something dirty to you?"

She blushes, her eyes darting to the floor, and bites her lower lip. "Ummm…"

Time to reel her back in, time to say something friendly or look pervy and blow it. I shrug. "I can't think of any other dirty sounding things I can say about your painting."

She turns to me with an amused expression and says, "How do you know it's my painting?"

"Because you're not admiring it. You look like you want to change something, fiddle with it."

"So do you."

"I'm the one who hung it here. So if it's cocked, then I didn't do a good job."

"It looks alright."

"That's just my point. We're not spectators admiring a piece of art in a gallery. Both of us are looking at your painting like it's our work."

"I hadn't thought of it like that."

"So it is your painting, right?"

Her smile widens so I forge ahead. "See, this painting over here" I gestured, "I didn't hang it and you didn't paint it, so we can go over there and admire it together." I touch her shoulder.

"How do you know I didn't paint this one, too?" she asks, falling into step with me.

I smile at her. "Because this one isn't as good as yours."

She laughs, finally. "I'm Fran."

"And I'm Eddie."

"So," she asks, as we make our way along the gallery wall, "Was the painting really cocked?"

"Well, the answer to that depends."

"On what?"

"Whether I get your phone number."

Our first date at an Italian place away from campus goes well, after I spend 20 minutes combing each strand of my hair into place before meeting her in front of the student union. We talk about her plans, her art, what she wants to be when she grows up and makes her impact on the world. I don't talk too much about changing light bulbs at the school, more about chemistry and metallurgy, and she's listening when I talk about the summer internship I spent extracting and smelting gold from junked computer parts at a reclamation plant. I try explaining to her why I like the work. How the impersonal challenge to formulate the best titration of chemicals is in fact a call to outwit and outsmart the immutable laws of physics. She nods and says that art is the same, it's all about getting as close to your ideal vision as you can. That's right, I say, and the little silence after that is comfortable and familiar instead of the stilted, awkward silences that sometimes happen on first dates when there will be no second. This quiet moment, shared during a plate of overcooked linguine, is when I fell for her.

It's on the second date, sitting on the steps of the gallery, enjoying the warm summer night when Fran spots the burn on my forearm, a souvenir from the sulfuric acid baths I set up to get the gold. She touches the wrinkled scar, running a nail over it, and I kiss her even though I wouldn't have a second earlier. She's into the kiss, our lips work together, hers moist, and we hold hands. I touch her red hair and the back of her neck, her skin soft and warm as we draw to each other. Her eyes closed, mine open.

Later that night in my apartment I touch the rest of her. Her nipples are the thinnest pink against her luminous white skin, and when I touch them too eagerly her breath catches and her forehead wrinkles and her nose scrunches up; I've gone too far too fast, gotten out of sync with her, and something about her scrunched up nose turns me on and melts my heart at the same time, and I kiss the tip of it and she giggles and then we're both laughing. Together.

*Over time that togetherness grows and we relax and I learn her, getting to know her mentally by touching her physically, the way her eyes close tight and her two front teeth show the slightest white against her lips when she's enjoying my touch and I feel like I've accomplished something, something more than just getting off or even getting her off, something greater than myself, this is what separates having sex from making love and in a way, it's the same challenge of getting as close as I can to the ideal, having her enjoy it, having her wanting it to match my wanting it. And it only gets better.*

*One night in the dead of winter we rush inside, into the warmth of the apartment we now share, and start kissing, fooling around, dropping our things and pulling off our winter jackets and boots as we heat up together. We have sex in the kitchen because we don't make it to the bedroom. The windows steam up and she shivers when I touch her with ice cold fingers. She'd been painting something with a bright blue acrylic paint which was still on her hands and the next morning I'm laughing to myself while she gets dressed. When she asks me what's so funny, I show her the blue streaks she'd left on my body and tell her I'd been having sex with Smurfette.*

*She fills out paperwork for schools, I help her assemble a portfolio and write an essay over a bottle of wine and Chinese takeout. That night we make love and I tell her that her work was good and any school would want to have her as much as I wanted to have her, and that I loved her. The next morning I mail her application on my walk to work. It gets rejected, and we send a few more a couple months later.*

*I finally graduate and my mom visits and the two sit to-gether in the auditorium while I collect my diploma. I take pictures of them both. At some point over dinner when Fran goes to the bathroom, my mother leans across the table and tells me that my father would have loved her, and that's why I'm teary when she returns and whispers "What's wrong?" and my mother winks at me.*

*Fran's father is a retired lawyer with a firm handshake and calluses like mine from working in his basement wood shop. I shake his hand when we take a trip out to her parent's for a Thanksgiving weekend. Her family is cozy and whole-some, her brother plays lacrosse and her mother makes the best turkey I've ever had, but the thing I'm taken with is her bedroom, preserved just as it must have been when she fin-ished high school, with stuffed animals on the bed and a van-ity mirror in the corner. I look through her yearbook and read the inscriptions. Fran tells me that her father worked from home and kept odd hours, sometimes working through the night, so she never got to christen the bed, not even with her old boyfriend Todd who'd drawn a heart on the back page. So we do, and joke about hearing a power saw whining through the floor as we finish.*

*The ring is good. My timing is bad. The ring is made out of titanium because any metallurgist knows that titanium shines brighter than silver, is stronger than steel, is more malleable than gold, and never tarnishes, all of which I think is a metaphor for love which I'm trying to articulate as I show her the ring. Fran takes it, says "Oh Eddie" and starts to cry. She says she loves me but she doesn't say yes and she shows me an acceptance letter from one of those schools she'd applied to months earlier. It's bitter and ironic that she's* been rejected by her safety school right across town; I could have dropped her off on my way to work, but her dream school has admitted her. Her dream school is an art institute in New Zealand. I'm quiet as I feel a void open somewhere inside, but then I tell that she has to go and she says that she has to stay so I tell her she has to go, and somehow we end up fighting, screaming at each other, both of us so determined to make the other happy that now we're miserable.

The day before she leaves almost everything is moved out. The place has magically transformed from our home back to a shitty ground floor two bedroom apartment in a rotting triple decker in a questionable neighborhood. Her things have been shipped back to her folks, and I'm already moved into my new place.

"I got you something," she tells me nervously, holding out a package to me. I take it from her, the brown wrapping paper crinkling in my hands.

"What is it?" I ask, running my index finger over the seam where she'd taped the wrapped package closed.

"Something I want you to have."

"What is it Fran?" I regard her warily as I still touch the wrapping paper. Lately, everything we say to each other has layers to it. Will the contents of this package hurt me some more?

She says nothing, her arms folded under her breasts, so I rip open the paper. Inside is the painting, the one from the gallery.

"Great. I'll be able to auction it in twenty years. I'll tell people that 'I knew her, way back when.'"

"Please don't start."

"Start? Start what?"

*"Please Eddie."*

*Holding up the painting, I squint at it theatrically. "You know that it wasn't."*

*"What?"*

*I reach out to her. She comes to me, and I kiss her. "That painting. It wasn't—"*

*"Don't!"*

*"It wasn't cocked. It was perfectly level."*

*She starts to cry, and her hands cover her mouth so that it almost looks like she's yawning, one of those little things about her that I love.*

*I kiss her again.*

*We make love, but it isn't loving the way I've enjoyed and come to expect without taking for granted; instead, it's the way I'd imagine the last meal of a condemned prisoner must be—no matter how well cooked and how delicious, the taste and texture of the food isn't what's relevant and can't cover up the reality to follow.*

*We kiss, lick, rub, suck, tease, squeeze, please; grunting, moaning, panting, gasping, grasping, inhaling, expelling and finally holding each other, sweaty from the press and the crush, breathing each other's breath all for the last time.*

*At some point the sky lightens and I hear a car horn outside. A yellow cab.*

*Fran leans close, so I feel her lips against the peach fuzz on my ear. "I knew it wasn't cocked."*

*Then she kisses me, and then she's gone.*

Art awoke.

Coughing, he sat up on the bench and he touched his face, cheeks sticky with drying tears. He rubbed at the slurry in his eyes smearing his vision, rubbed until he could see straight. Staring at the ground in front of him, he leaned forward, his back cracking as he sat up straight.

"Dude," he said, turning to Ray. "That was … I can't even say what."

Ray said nothing.

"Worth every penny." Art nudged him. "Ray?"

The hood of his sweatshirt fell back, revealing Ray's pale, slack face. His blue lips, parted, revealed his tongue, also blue, and a rope of drool slid out from the corner of his mouth. His glassy eyes shined wide at nothing.

"No," Art breathed, leaning towards him. Ray's body shifted and slid part way off the edge of the bench, his knees scraping the leaves on the ground.

At age nine, Art spent a Christmas with his cousin who lived upstate, out in the woods. Behind his cousin's house was a scrubby polluted pond that looked idyllic, surrounded by trees all dusted with a crust of snow. When she heard them preparing to go outside, boots dragging across the vestibule floor his aunt called out "Stay off the lake, like I told yooz," without looking up from The Price is Right. The two went outside, crunched their way through the snow covering his cousin's yard and along the short path to the lake itself. They stared at the wan sun, and at the glare it made on the frozen water. Then Art took a shaky step down, balancing himself against the shore with a tree branch he found. He shuffled a few paces across the perfectly smooth, clean ice and turned. He slipped and almost busted his ass, moon walking to catch himself. From the shore, his cousin snorted with laughter.

"Why don't you come here and laugh in my face, moth-erfucker?" He yelled, liking the echoes.

"Cause I'm not a crazy fuck, like you!" his cousin called back.

Art called him a pussy and slid out a few more feet. The ice below him sighed and cracked, a gunshot in the stillness. Art's breath caught in his throat. Pulse pounding, his body went ramrod straight and stiff. Suddenly burning hot with tension, a drop of sweat rolled into his eye, and after a long, unquantifiable time of staring at the spider web of cracked ice beneath his feet, waiting, waiting for something to happen, he slowly, timidly stepped back toward the shore, toward his cousin, now watching him, wide eyed.

The lake surface here felt solid, so he shifted his weight onto the stepping foot. Nothing. He stepped again, another mincing step toward solid ground, toward land, and again, nothing. He let out the breath he'd been holding for so long that he couldn't remember taking it and inhaled a fresh blast of cold air. Some of his tension faded as Art relaxed a hair.

The ice gave way.

Art let out a short scream that lasted until he submerged, the freezing water going right down his gullet through his open mouth, running up the cuffs of his pants, through his shirt, soaking everything, the gray iron water so cold it didn't even feel cold, just shocking. Art thrashed around. He sank into the frigid mud at the bottom, kicking up dirt and filthy sediment so thick it blotted out the sunlight and he couldn't tell which direction was up, so he thrashed harder, twisting and corkscrewing himself further and further into his clothes which bound and tied him up, so that finally he lay in the muck, punching and kicking until he gasped for breath. The cold water flooded in. Now the cold inside him matched the cold of the lake outside him, and Art weakened further, his struggles feeble as his time stretched out, as each softer and softer thump of his balled fist against the sticky, yielding mud took longer and longer, became more and more epic in fuzzier and fuzzier slow motion. Too tired to panic anymore he had one last lucid thought, "This isn't too bad," before the blackness took him.

He didn't remember the ambulance crew his cousin summoned, being pronounced dead, the epinephrine shot that restarted his heart, or the coma; he remembered only the cold, the terror, the dark. The grogginess as he woke up in the hospital two days later, for once glad to see his father and mother, was worlds away.

"No," Art repeated, "no, no, no." He slapped at Ray's chest, and put his face close to Ray's, hoping to feel breath, but when Ray's clammy corpse slid the rest of the way off the bench, Art gave up.

He stood, his stomach lurching, leaned against the fence and vomited onto the bike path until the roiling queasiness subsided. He fumbled for his keys and dropped them twice in the slimy leaves attempting to unlock his bicycle.

He looked back at Ray, the terror junkie who'd now gone the route most terror junkies went, lying dead in front of the bench having finally scared himself to death. At his feet, the twonky lay upside down. Art went over and retrieved it, frowning. He didn't kid himself that this was noble or what Ray would have wanted, but Ray was dead and he needed it.

So he took it.

Art pushed his bicycle, too shaken to ride it. It was chilly outside. He needed home. Fran would warm him up. Fran could massage his shoulders or … at least she could listen to him talk about this, Fran listened to him, but … Fran … Is Fran? Was Fran? Was he? Is he?

"Good Times" originally appeared in *Bastion Magazine.*

# Liberty Motel
by Larry Malchow

I hallucinate. That much I admit. I see things that aren't really there, much of it crazy, some scary or haunting. I always have. Always will, I guess. It's my curse. I've grown used to it, though, so I don't medicate anymore. Meds made me forget real things that were there, so I have lost much of my life to them. The visions eventually pass anyway. Once I got over fearing them, I frankly found them entertaining. My life can be like paying to see a movie but also getting to see a second one at the same time. Or many. And I never know what I will see, or when, so it's always interesting, and there are surprises. At my age, all I really have left are surprises. There is not much else to really see in this empty desert, anyway.

You know the drill. I know the drill. Everyone knows it. A friend invites you down to help, then you're trapped in his smoke and mirrors universe. I just need you to do this. Then that. And this other thing. It goes on and on like a dark, narrowing tunnel. Before you know it, you learn he is terminal and you inherit his kingdom, and the blind tunnel goes on forever. You can't leave because—*goddammit!*— there is no one else and you still have a conscience. Then you think, *Why not? I have nothing else.* Before long you start liking it. You are seeing new things in the darkness, and your new prison starts looking like freedom. No place else to go, anyway. You fled your past after it fled you, and you can't remember much of it. It does bother you, but you decide that both reality and imagination are things we create ourselves. And you can make more of both every day.

So Sokolove gets the hiccups and nearly chokes himself to death on his phlegm while I am cleaning his oxygen tank breathing tube with boiled water and vinegar to destroy any bacteria that might be fermenting in there. I disinfect my own CPAP this way (we all deserve to breathe freely, even the middle-aged and no longer useful). The sixteen year-old Mexican girl has peeled back Sokolove's blue comforter and is changing his filthy sheets. Her movements are so fluid, she looks like a great lake with flowing tributaries for limbs, water rushing everywhere. Since we don't have housekeeping staff, I'm glad to pay minimum wage for this temporary help from Lake Ximena, one of our residents. And Great Lakes kids need cash too. This is not a money-making concern anyway. Our operating budget is as much on its death bed as Sokolove is.

She takes a swig of her *Nestle Pure Life* bottled water, adding more fluid to her system of bubbling streams and canals. She always has a bottle with her. Reminds me of my ex who couldn't smoke unless she had a sweet drink at hand, my lovely wife who navigated life from her center of gravity ass and directed the show from her premium seat with seat of the pants discernment. The wife at least I think I had. I am not really sure if those I remember were real flesh and blood.

*Ximena,* Sokolove manages through his phlegmy, lung-rattling cough. *Do that magic thing again, you know, with your tongue.*

*No.*

*Come on. I want to see it. It's trippy.*

*I am not a circus clown, Mister Hiccup. I'm a little girl—* She licks her finger, then pokes her thrust out butt with a sizzling sound—*going on hotness.* Now she looks like a tongue of fire.

*Okay then, tell me what you want to be when you grow up and get tits. I'm bored.*

*Jesus, Sokolove,* I say, *she's just a kid. Enough with the tits. Read a book or something. Damn.*

*What do you care?*

*I had a daughter. I was always on watch for predators.*

*You never had kids.*

*I think I did.*

*You never married.*

*I might have.*

Ximena says, *A beautiful actress married to a younger Tom Cruise. It's in the genes.* Points to her butt again. *And the jeans.* She is now a twirling mitochondrial helix increasing speed while fluffing the pillows. *And the stars, Mister Hiccup. It's in the stars.* She is a constellation of pulsing stars. I am not sure which one. Maybe all of them.

*Girls in America are now taught they can be anything, Ximena,* I tell her.

*And boys can't?*

*Boys are taught they have to be … something. It's different.*

*I don't understand.*

*Me neither.*

*Come on,* Sokolove urges between hiccups. *Don't be a snotty wench. Do that trippy thing for your old pal.*

*Old, yes. Pal, I don't know … Pay up first. And I am not a wench, whatever that means.*

Sokolove holds up a worn, wrinkled buck, and she flows toward him and swamps it. Then she thrusts her face right up to his and touches her nose with her tongue. Only ten percent of people can do that. I looked it up. It's a genetic connective tissue disorder. I see her tongue elongate and twirl itself up toward the ceiling. A snake. But I suspect that really isn't happening. Sokolove laughs through his hollow death rattle.

*You're a freak, Ximena, just like your pal Sokolove here.*

*Yeah, you got any talents besides being wrinkly and old?*

*Those are smile lines, dear, or laugh lines, technically na-solabial folds, defined facial structures that run from the corners of your nose to corners of your lips that support the bruccal fat pad. The lines deepen from a lifetime of smiling kindly at people. Get smart about shit before being a smartass.*

*Whatever. You got any skills besides running drugs or people across the border?*

*Shut your little pretty mouth or someday someone will hear you, and go get your little brother. I want to see him turn into a lizard again.* Miguel can flip his eyelids inside out without touching them. He has *Floppy Eye Syndrome.* His eyelids even evert on their own while he sleeps. First time I saw him do it, my metaphorical brain turned him into a demented Komodo dragon with teeth. But that's just me. I am Mulder. I see demons everywhere. I live the *X-Files*.

*I might be a smartass, but you are a shitass, Mister Hiccup,* Ximena says.

*But an endearing one.*

*Yes, an endearing one.* She waters his dying Spider Plant from her water bottle. It looks to me like the water pours from her hand. *I will save this planet yet,* she says almost to herself.

*Plant,* I say. *Not planet.*

*Plant.*

*Besides,* Sokolove says, *your whole family is a freakshow, you said so yourself.*

Ximena sticks out her tongue. I see it slap his face silly before rolling back up into her mouth like a retracting carpet. *I'm going to make Miguel charge you two bucks,* she says, *and I get half, just for your disrespect.*

*Good.* He laughs. *I'll pay. We don't have cable. It's cheap entertainment.*

This time Sokolove's laugh almost blows out a heart valve. He has emphysema and congestive heart failure from a lifetime habit of inhaling two packs of forest fire per day. *Mavericks.* The brand of real men and cowboys. My eyeballs often dress him in a Stetson and cowboy boots. My friend doesn't have long for this world and doesn't know if there will be a next one, but we all like to think there is one, don't we? I know he secretly does despite his denials. He is always planning his next move. His next place will always be better. He won't be smoking there, though, and I no longer allow him to smoke here either. We've spit too much smoke into our world from our scumbag brains.

Ximena finishes, grabs her water, and walks out, blowing Sokolove a kiss, then flips him the bird. I see her lips fly through the air and absorb into his cheeks. Her finger spanks his nose before flying back to her hand. She smiles. Ximena really does like the old, cranky bastard. She knows he is saving her family from a dreary life of want in Mexico.

I reconnect his hose to a fresh oxygen tank so he can breathe. *Thanks, Smitty.*

*You don't sound good today, buddy.* The more he teases Ximena, I know, the worse he feels, as if he wants to cram in all his teasing before our very life-giving atmosphere smothers him.

*Fuck that,* he says. *I'm fine. It's our American melting pot that's on life support.*

He need not say it. I can read his eyes. He is on his last legs. Sometimes I see only a skeleton in his chair, even while he is telling me he is glad I came to take over. Somebody must, he says. This is the motel of the free and home of the brave.


It's a twelve-room broken down rectangle of a building from the fifties with peeling green paint and a Lady Liberty sign that no longer lights up at night. The *Liberty Motel* looks like an ancient dinosaur carcass sprawled on its belly in the dust as if ready to give up the ghost and go extinct, join the other vestiges of the past in the boneyard, the café next door, and *Sinclair* gas station down the road, the one with the Brontosaurus logo. What was once a highway artery that brought in tourists is now only a ghostly, blue vein of road just a mile from the border that is traveled only by those who are lost. Or illegal. Everybody now takes the I-5 to the west, the major north-south route from San Diego to Tijuana. And back.

That's good in one way. Remoteness has its advantages for our niche business, though we always have empty rooms because the highway stole our traffic. We take *the tired, poor, huddled masses yearning to breathe free*, even if Sokolove can't without an oxygen tank. Then we give them shelter until Allen Gamble can get the fake IDs and take them north. You have no hope these days without papers. Ximena's family is destined for an egg farm in Utah where they don't ask new employees any difficult questions if they keep their heads down and keep pumping out unfertilized eggs for America's belly. Sokolove instructs them not to go out alone at night except for the person on watch who climbs up on the roof. Coyotes might be the interlopers, but they think we are. They travel in hungry packs around here.

Ximena, ten year-old Miguel, and their parents, Manuel and Guadalupe, have been here for a week waiting for Gamble. I have to admit I like them. Manuel can fix anything. Sometimes I see him as Father Time, sometimes the North Wind. He is a little gray to have such young kids. Today he's tacking fresh shingles onto the flat roof to keep the rain out, not that it rains much, but when it does, it pours. Guadalupe heals. She concocted a paste from desert plants that finally closed the festering sore in Sokolove's nostrils, dried from the desert air and rubbed raw from his breathing tube. I always see her angel wings. They are the only family we currently harbor from immigration authorities. Other than the rooms they occupy, we only have three regulars who pay a special monthly rate. The other units sit empty. I have Ximena vacuum and change the sheets anyway. Best to stay on top of the Black Widow situation. Patrol daily and squash any interlopers before they can claim their turf, spin chaotic webs, and take you out with their venom. We don't want our guests to get bitten.

We don't see our other regulars except to collect the rent or for housekeeping. Young Pena is probably a dealer. He only comes and goes in the dead of night like a vampire and has no visitors. He is so dark you can't even see his face unless there is moonlight, but I see his long and pointy vampire fangs. A fat Mexican lady, Maria, is the recluse in number three. She has spooky black eyes and licks her lips often. In her eyes I see dark, desolate planets that don't look like ours. The third tenant is a swarthy disabled vet, Angel, who we only see when he drives off or returns in his beater *Ford Probe* with quarts in paper bags. His face looks as empty as the unused rooms. Must be a congenial dude, though. He also delivers supplies to Maria and makes a run for us when we ask.

*They all just want to be left alone, so leave them alone,* Sokolove told me when I arrived. *Everybody hides from something. Or runs from it.* So I just let them be. My job is easy. I receive the illegals from Mateo Reyes and harbor them until Gamble retrieves them. I hide them when Agent Calloway comes sniffing around. Not sure if he is border patrol or immigration. Don't care. I do know he's a dick. When my eyeballs land on him, his stubby neck and fat skull look like a giant penis, except he has two little, beady eyes instead of just one in the middle. Otherwise, I just pay the bills and keep the place clean. And keep my eyeballs pasted on the horizon. On this blue road, you can see a car heading south toward us from almost forever.

110

The only tough part is staying open. We must manage with just three paying tenants. Apparently, the itinerants pay Reyes and Gamble, and for their room and board we only get a nominal fee, an Andrew Jackson for every day no matter how many rooms they use or family members eat our southwest chili and sandwiches. I have no clue where they get the money. They don't look affluent. If they were, why come here? Why not just stay in Mexico? Rich Americans bail out to expatriate there all the time, which is ironic when you consider all the illegals trying to come here to make a living. I should ask Reyes how all this works when I see him. I'm new here, and this is my first family of illegals. Glad we get the green, though. Helps pay for the lights and AC. Without AC, this desert would dry us up and turn us to dust.

I haven't yet met either Reyes or Gamble. Reyes used to run pot with Sokolove. He's the guy who digs the tunnels. It's the only way across these days since they erected the wall and funded those fleets of coastal patrol boats, choppers, and airplanes to shut down the sky and ocean corridors. Maybe I'll just keep my mouth shut, though. The less I know, the safer I am. And the fewer strange visions I'll have.

Ximena is sorting dirty laundry in the utility room when I bring in her wages. She stops to sip her designer water. It floods into Lake Ximena.

*You know,* I tell her, *he doesn't do this for profit. He's really a good guy.*

*Why does he do it?*

*Not sure. He's a free thinker, I guess.*

*What does that mean? Free from what?*

I don't want to say, unsure I can articulate the whole thing right. My brain is better with pictures than words. *Standard notions of right and wrong maybe.*

*Why do YOU do it?*

*He's dying. I'm the next man up.*

*Who says?*

*Me.*

*You both are good people,* she says soberly.

*How do you know that?*

*Woman's intuition.*

*I wouldn't trust that if I were you. It's superstition.*

*At least it's not regular stition.*

*He's right. You are a smartass.*

She looks serious. Like her mother. *Why not? You give people a new life, don't you? That makes you good. Lots of you people in this strange place are good people.*

*What people? What strange place? We're only a mile from your homeland.*

*Never mind,* she says. She turns to Sokolove's stained boxers. She needs to *Shout* the stains out. *He's a little short in hygiene, though. A shitass. Literally.*

*He has challenges. We all do.*

*What did you mean,* she asks, *that girls can do anything but boys have to do something?*

*Never mind. I see shit that isn't there. And I babble about it.*

*No. Tell me.*

*Look, I know women have had it tough for lots of reasons, in America and everywhere else, and we're all focused on that these days, but when you come down to it, boys must*

112

go out into the world and do something, normally stuff they don't want to do, just to survive. Because life is not a Disney film. Girls? They can do that if they want, but they can also choose to stay home and bring children across the threshold of their bodies into this world we live on. Create new life. It's a choice boys don't have. We can raise them, but we can't feed them with our bodies, protect them while they're gestating, and usher them into this fucked up life. We're not as ... whole or complete as you, and never can be.

*You want to have a baby, Mister Smitty?*

I envision myself giving birth on a table covered with white cloth. The baby ejects from between my thighs, plunging into a universe of swirling chaos, inanimate things like medical instruments and surgical masks flying about the room on their lonesome. *Jesus. No.*

*But I get it. I do.*

*You do?*

*Yes.*

*Good. Because I don't.*

I head to the office and think about that, not the hygiene or the babies or chaotic universe, the motivation. Why do I do this? You wouldn't know it from his trade, but Sokolove is not like me. He's a political beast, not a master criminal. He never really ran drugs or people to get rich. For him it's as much a political statement as blowing up shit for a terrorist. Sokolove simply does not believe that human beings should be denied good pot by a government or that government should keep people out who want in. In fact, he doesn't believe in government or codified laws at all. If a guy assaults you, Sokolove thinks you should kill him. One less problem in his mind, for you, for others, for everyone.

People would then behave better. Let freedom ring, baby. Not sure if that is libertarian or what, but it's Sokolove. Sitting at my office desk, I can see him bleeding out of the paisley wallpaper with six guns blazing, still in his wheel chair, still breathing oxygen from a tank through a tube. It doesn't help me determine why I am here, but I think I know anyway. I am as much itinerant as Ximena's family, a gray, thirsty Bedouin in the neon land of the red, white, and blue.

Even though he might harass the shit out of them, Sokolove has a special soft spot for illegal aliens. He himself was shuttled between foster homes during his formative years. He understands why people might have to move very far to find the American dream. He never found it himself, but he knows this country is really a different place than Americans in the suburbs see. He thinks I am quite normal and they are the ones with weird visions.

I met the guy back when I was dealing weed on the streets of San Diego. I had a nice niche amongst the chic twentysomethings in the Balboa Park area up University Avenue. Yuppies and students like to climb their rope and see strange shit too when it suits them. They just have to pay for it. Sokolove was the runner for my main supplier, this tattooed circus freak named Sylvia who fed me with primo Central American ganja. I happened to arrive at her apartment the day she OD'd on *Mexican Mud.* I ran into Sokolove in the parking lot while paramedics were removing her cartooned body. She dipped too deep into the deep. She had to move on to the next somewhere, a place we all must go to blind.

From then on, we just cut out the middle tattooed circus freak and dealt with each other face to face. After the gangs shut us down we decided we best find another profession if we were still interested in living inside our skin. Sokolove said we should run warm bodies north from the Baja to freedom instead. Not having honed another skill besides dealing, I was all in. Why not? Those folks just want a better life. But now that he's dying, I guess it's my turn to step up and become the main man. When I look at Sokolove, mostly I see just a broken old man in a wheelchair struggling to suck atmosphere into his lungs. I'm pretty sure that much is real.

And why not step up? What else is left for me? I have fought their wars and played the good corporatist. Of that I'm pretty sure. I have raised their red-blooded American children as my legacy to this nation of shakers and movers, or at least think I did. I paid their taxes for infrastructure and better weapons. Probably. I have followed their laws. I don't recall ever landing in jail. It was only after my divorce and estrangement of the kids I think I made that I turned to the bottle and lost my job, alcohol lending a new darkness to my visions. Peddling weed is just something that turned up—a mid-life crisis, if you will—that I did for survival, then Sokolove turned up too. Maybe I have earned my right to drop off the grid and manage this motel. Anyway, I took the job because Sokolove needs me. My buddy is fading fast, soon to leave me alone in a desolate world where I see things that are really there and things that might not be. But I chose to live in this no man's land. I am no man's victim.

Manuel and Guadalupe are standing near the Lady Liberty sign engaged in animated conversation. That wobbly sign is propped up by an unstable frame. Gusting Santa Ana winds keep knocking it down. A few days ago, I found it resting against the lone Desert Willow and cluster of Prickly Pear near the road. That single willow must absorb and sequester over a ton of carbon dioxide in its lifetime. What would we breathe without trees like that sucking up $CO_2$ and spitting out breathable air? What would Sokolove breathe? The thick hide of that cactus is able to retain water the dry air strives to reclaim. If only people had thick skins like that, I think. We wouldn't die of thirst in this godforsaken landscape. The cactus is a chlorophyll machine too and spits oxygen into our faces. The willow looks like a lone sentry on watch for Calloway and his minions, the cactus like a massive bed of fruit that might nourish us with its juices while we await Gamble's arrival.

I know the parents are worried they have been here too long, that Calloway might show up again soon. Last time I had the family hide in the crawl space in the office back room. It was a tight, sweaty fit for the half hour the agent grilled me. They looked like a ball of human twine in there that wound itself tight by playing *Twister*. Fortunately, Calloway was alone that day and not in the mood to sweat out all his internal fluids ransacking the premises for illegals.

I'm not really used to this yet, but the whole family strikes me as odd. They don't talk much except amongst themselves as if they are plotting something. Ximena can touch her nose with her tongue and Miguel flip his eyelids inside out with no hands. Those are two rare abilities for a small family. But Sokolove thinks there is more. He thinks

Ximena's parents have perfected weird talents too, and he's chomping at the bit to know what. Like he says, we have no cable. And I wonder if all the future illegals I house will have their own unique skills. Is that what you develop when you're poor and have no TV or computer? What do you do for entertainment? It's weird stuff, but what else is there out here besides inside out eyelids and tongues touching noses? No *Dish* here either. I am the only one here who sees freaky visions without being gouged for a monthly fee.

Ximena finds me in the office playing solitaire on the old computer. It's fun for me because the face cards always mutate from royalty to stick people to bloodthirsty aliens to pretty birds flying away to freedom.

*Done,* she says.

*Thank you for doing things right,* I say.

*Why? You know people who don't?*

Again, seems like an odd question. *Don't you? Who in this world does things the right way?*

*Everybody I know. We learned the hard way.*

*What do you mean? Where are you from, anyway?*

*Never mind, but all my people back there are just like me. Hospital corners for the bed sheets. Fabric softener in the laundry. Vinegar for the tile floor.*

*All work in housekeeping?*

*You just don't get it, Mister Smitty. Not just housekeeping.* She pokes her painted and charmed forefinger nail at my temple. *I'm trying to get into your thick skull that when we do things, we do them right. Not sloppy like people in this land of water. Leenowlee!*

*Leenowlee. That's not Spanish.* I took Spanish in high school. My buddies and I learned all the insults on our own. *Me cago en tu madre. That's Spanish.*

*Nice. I shit on your mother. Never mind, Leenowlee.*

Leenowlee? Land of water? She must come from the most parched boondocks in the central mountain regions. Maybe a desert worse even than this. The dark world I see in Maria's eyes.

Manuel and Guadalupe are transforming unit ten, both climbing up ladders to do their jobs. They look like moths climbing the walls. He tears the moldy wallpaper out, and she paints the walls a pure, clean white. What a whirlwind of industry. Their wings flutter when they move. No wonder Americans want these folks on their payroll, especially if it's under the table.

I see Ximena again when she checks on Sokolove. She brings in his plate of fajitas and black beans, sets it down on his tray, and kisses him gently on the forehead. She then brushes his shaggy hair back over his ears with her fingers and uses a tissue to wipe a small snot bubble from his nose. Sokolove has just told me that Reyes called. Another family will arrive any day. Luckily, we have room. Ximena waters the houseplant that looks like it is on life support too, then she traps a Luna Moth she sees climbing the wallpaper. She cups it in her hands, walks to the door and frees it in the external world. I see an entire family of moths flee to safety. They are a swirl of winged snowflakes flying horizontally north. Then she applies her mother's paste to Sokolove's nose. *How you be, Gordito?* she asks him in a whisper. Gordito. Chubby.

Sokolove smiles and slaps her ass.

*Sokolove, no! That's not okay.*

*I'm only human,* he pleads.

*You're a human piggy, Gordito,* she says, then flops on the bed.

Sokolove starts shoveling food, dropping lettuce and cheese on his shirt. *Touch your nose with your tongue for me, my little cheesecake,* he teases.

*No.*

*Tell us, what freaky shit can your moms and pops do?*

*None of your beeswax, Porky Pig Man.*

*Come on. I'm bored. Tell me.*

I say, *Sokolove, stop badgering. You're lucky she likes you and brings you food and comes by to see if you're still sucking air. She's a good kid.*

He hangs his head. *Yeah, I know. I'm just bored.*

*Papa,* she says quietly, *can sing, and Momma dance.*

*That's not so weird,* Sokolove challenges.

*It's how they do it, Mister Sowbelly.*

*Okay. Okay. Would love to see it, Wicked Teen Witch of the West.*

*I am the beautiful teen witch of the North Star, Mister Swine Snout.* Then she says, *Maybe, before we leave. When will that be, Mister Smitty?*

*Wish I knew, dear.* I notice Sokolove really does have the snout of a swine. And this young girl is certainly beautiful. Perhaps both things are real.

The dry, sixty mile per hour Santa Anas have knocked the motel sign down again. I am out there standing it up when the two black *Ford Expeditions* with tinted windows roll in, kicking up dust that invades my eyes. The men in white shirts and sunglasses jump out. For a moment, they are black and white *Teenage Mutant Ninja Turtles*, then black dominoes with white dots, each a different number. All wear gold badges. Who else? Calloway. A turtle head penis with no neck, then a domino phallus in shades.

*Mister Schmidt.*

*Mister Calloway.*

*Special Agent.*

*Agent.*

*SPECIAL Agent.*

*Especially an Agent Calloway.*

*I need to check your rooms, asshole.*

*Have at it.*

*I know what you people do here, cowboy.* But I see he is the one in chaps and spurs, at least for a flickering instant. He motions to his skein of black and white ducks, his hand swirling purple air as if punching bruises into the world.

*Good. At least someone does.*

The men fan out, now black and white feathers of a giant peacock. I am not worried. One of the four family members is always on watch scanning the road with binoculars. Little Miguel loves that job. Makes him feel like *Especially an Agent* Miguel or something.

They barge into the rooms. Most are unlocked and empty for housekeeping. Pena is naked in bed. A seal. *Hey, man! What?* Angel is drinking in bed too, mariachi music on AM radio. He is a gigantic and black *Jack Daniels* label who just waves weakly at the agent in sunglasses who bursts in and checks the bathroom. Maria cuts loose with a stream of Spanish invective. For the moment, she is simply rather large Maria. Sokolove gives Calloway the finger from the threshold of Unit One. *Fuck you,* he ekes through his phlegm.

*Why don't you just die, maggot?* Calloway asks.

*You first,* Sokolove manages.

No one else is home. There might be residents living in other rooms, but there is no evidence of their occupation.

*I'll be back, Mister Shit.*

*Do that, Terminator,* I say. *Mi casa, su casa.* For a moment, he really is Arnold Schwarzenegger. Shaped like a big penis.

The men hop in their cars and tear off. I eat their dust. It's worse than the merciless Santa Anas. I really need a cool drink of water.

Angel returns from the supply run I sent him on. He gets reduced rent for doing it. This way I can stay here and keep my inventive eye on things. Ximena loads the groceries into the fridge. *Alien 3* is playing on the old TV in the office adjacent to the kitchen. We don't have many disks, and it's one of my favorites because of the gritty world it depicts, so I play that one over and over. Ripley is swan diving backwards from a pedestal into a vat of molten something while a vicious papoose alien bursts through her abdomen and shrieks hello to the world.

*You watch nasty movies, Mister Smitty. All the creatures from space are ugly and mean. I think you people have a lot of fear.*

*We people?*

*You people.*

She drops the greens into the fridge humidity drawer. The celery and tomatoes have faces too (you say *tomato*, I say red-faced baseball with a smiley face). *Many do*, I say. *What's that you're holding?*

*A card game. Settlers of Catan. Miguel and I are going to teach Mister Pigheaded how to play.*

*What kind of game is it?*

*You know, you settle land and acquire resources, and build wealth.*

*Oh. Life in America.*

*If you say so. Do you play games?*

*I play searching for Atlantis.*

*What's that, Atlantis?*

*A water kingdom.*

*It's real?*

*The searching is.*

*I don't understand you, Mister Smitty.*

*That's okay. I don't either.*

She takes a deep swallow of water. I am now sure she is really Lake Michigan, standing upright and connecting to other great bodies of water. *Mister Smitty, I think you need a girlfriend.*

*I think I had lots. Or they had me. Either way, I know I've been had.*

*I don't understand your expressions.*

*Expressions are hard to read.*

*People too*, she says.

I know our regulars want to be left alone, but I feel I should check in with them at least weekly to ensure their needs are satisfied. Perhaps I can provide a few small, inexpensive services or niceties that will make their stays more comfortable and keep them as tenants longer. If we can't, I don't know how we can pay the mounting bills. Angel seems the most approachable, so I knock on the door of Unit Four.

He answers the door naked but for a pair of tattered jean shorts and a half-empty quart of *Jack* his right hand holds by the neck.

*Yeah?*

*Can I come in? I'd like to talk.*

*Kay.*

He motions to the desk chair and collapses onto the bed. He might look tired, but he has none of the telltale signs of being half in the bag. My brain forms an entire ocean beach behind him. Angel is lounging in the shade of a palapa holding hands with his best, true love, a quart of *Jack Daniels*.

*What up?* he asks.

He doesn't seem very interested in small talk, so I just come out and ask if he is happy with his current accommodations and if there is anything I can do to make him more comfortable.

*I don't need much,* he says. *I just like my peace and quiet, but it's nice of you to ask.*

*How long have you been with us?*

*Not sure. Seems like forever. I'm not used to such long days.*

*Not sure I understand.*

*It's just the way things work.*

*Oh. Will you let me know if I can do anything for you?*

*Probably not.*

A Mexican family is playing beach volleyball behind him, a mother and father and daughter and son. Instead of the bottle, Angel is holding up one side of the net. A ball bounces off his head and back into play. He does not notice. The children are laughing gleefully at the ball's ricochet back into the air and over the net. I thank Angel for seeing me and tell him I am always available should he need anything. *I won't,* he says.

On my way out I ask him why he likes living at the Liberty Motel.

*This is where I belong,* he says.

Like most things around here, like most things in my life, I am not sure what that means.

Since it is afternoon, I then take my chances that Pena will be up and about. I knock on his door, and he answers immediately. *Please come in,* he courteously offers without me saying a word. I sit at his desk while he takes a seat on the edge of the bed. *How are you?* he asks as if he is the motel manager and me the guest. *Do you like it here?*

*Yes,* I tell him.

We talk for an hour, mainly about me. Pena is full of questions about my life. I am not having visions while we talk and don't know why. Today he does not look like a vampire. He has normal teeth. Pena has a calming effect on my mind. Finally, he says, *I hope I'm not a bother to anyone.*

*God, no.*

*That is an interesting expression, Mister Schmidt, invoking God. Many people do that. Why?*

I am afraid I might have offended him. Mexicans are some of the most passionate Catholics in the world. *I'm not sure, really. I never thought about it.*

*It seems a sort of invocation of the other-worldly, some-
times out of astonishment or even a milder form of surprise,
sometimes for emphasis, perhaps sometimes a plea for help
from a greater power.*

I don't know what to say. I don't know where he is going with this. *You're probably right. It is a very flexible word.*

*I have had much time to think since I have been here,* he
offers, *and I find such exclamations most curious.*

I am finding him most curious. Sylvia was the only other drug dealer I knew. The tattooed circus lady didn't talk
like this.

*I will let you know if I come to any further understand-
ings on this,* he says.

I thank him for that and decide this would be a good
time to leave because he has become a priest surrounded by
sheep. One strays, and he guides it back to the flock with a
simple wave of his wrist.

*Just let me know if you need anything, Pena.*

*Certainly, Mr. Schmidt. And please let me know if you
do.*

I am somewhat disconcerted and not sure I am ready to
face distant and sometimes surly Maria, but I am resolved
to check in with her anyway. When I arrive at Unit 8, her
door is open despite the heat, the AC off. She is propped up
in her bed reading a magazine. There are stacks of magazines everywhere. I greet her in Spanish.

*I speak English,* she says. She must. The magazines are
in English. They are of all types: news, fluffy entertainment
like *People,* a few good literary publications, some deeper
political magazines. *Smithsonian.* This woman has eclectic,
and not simple, taste. I settle into the desk chair.

*I know you will ask if I need anything, but I don't,* she informs me without looking up from her reading. *My sons see to all my needs.*

*Sons?*

*Angel and Pena.*

*Wow. I didn't know. They don't look alike.*

*They are.*

*They don't look like you.*

*They are.*

*Huh.*

*We are the first family Mr. Sokolove helped. We decided to stay. We like it here.*

*Oh. Good.*

*Thank you for visiting me,* she says curtly. I don't know why, but she looks like a giant hen propped in a nest cluck-clucking over her brood.

But of course, I am not sure if any of these chats really occurred.

I am sure of Sokolove, though. And Ximena. They are playing their card game in Unit One. A third player has cards, but the chair is empty. *Where is Miguel?* I ask.

*On watch on the roof,* Ximena says. *I am playing for him.*

*She is cheating her little brother,* Sokolove insists.

*I do not cheat. You shitsack liar, Mister shit for brains.*

*It's lying sack of shit,* Sokolove insists. *At least let me teach you how to swear right. You got the shit for brains part, though.*

*You want to play for him, Mister Smitty?*

*No, thanks. I get enough fantasy just looking through my eyeballs every day.* But at the moment I am relieved to be seeing nothing unusual.

*I think, Mister Smitty, that you should learn to like being different. If everything in the stew is just meat and no vegetables or gravy, the stew is boring and does not taste so good.*

*The little cheesecake might be onto something, Smitty.*

*I'll take it under advisement. I had my first long chat with the regulars, Maria, Pena, and Angel.*

*Good souls, huh?* Sokolove asks.

*Yeah. Maybe a little strange. Or I am.*

*Like the little lady says, Smitty, every ingredient in the stew is different.*

*Yeah. I'm just not sure what veggie I am.*

*Mister Smitty,* Ximena says, *isn't this obvious? You are the new chef in the kitchen.*

I guess I add the spices and blend us all together, then I just watch it all simmer.

*Lenowlee!* She admonishes.


It is after midnight. I am at my office desk gazing at the paisley. A little boy emerges from the pattern. He looks like me. He is frowning, his eyes dropping to the floor. I know I have disappointed him. A haughty teen girl pushes him to get moving. She looks my way with disdain. Their mother appears, an older and more ill-tempered version of the irritated girl, sitting in a chair. She sips from a *Snapple* and smokes an *Eve.* I see the hate for me in her eyes.

Now the boy is a young man wearing a necktie, looking even more like I once did. An older man at the office has his finger in the young man's face, bullying him with words.

He fades, and the irritable girl is standing in a living room looking irritated with another man. She is swept away by the gray woman holding a Snapple in one hand and cigarette in the other. She sits on her ass staring at me. Her hate bores into my skull.

They could simply be an undigested bit of beef, a crumb of cheese, or fragment of undone potato. They might be more gravy than grave. Doesn't matter. These ghosts scare me. I see enough of my past to know I don't want a Grim Reaper in a cowl to point to my future with its bony finger. I leap from my chair, but I am too late. I see my skull baking in the desert sun on the cracked earth of a dried-up oasis. I flee.

I find Ximena up on the roof in a lawn chair with binoculars and a water bottle. I sit in the second chair. *See anything interesting?*

*Stars.* She points. *That's Pisces. I'm Pisces.* I actually see the fish wriggling. It is not a fish in water. It IS water. *When you see it, Mister Smitty, think of me.*

*I will. I'm Aquarius.*

*When I see it, I will always remember you.*

*I'm not that important.*

*I think you are.*

*Thank you.* She unconsciously winds her hair around her forefinger. Rivers cross. The laser streams of Ghostbusters are crossing. They are beautiful, swirling jet streams on their way to everywhere, on their way even to sky.

*What did you do before this, Mister Smitty?*

*I don't really remember. I am a migrant of time. Lost to the Ages.*

*Mr. Sokolove says you see things.*

*I do, and I have. Not much worth seeing, though.*

*I would like to see things.*

*I wouldn't wish that on anyone.*

*You think you are cursed, Mister Smitty, but it is really your special gift. It makes you Mister Smitty.*

*Maybe.*

*You still have dreams, Mister Smitty? I do. I don't mean your visions. I mean things you want, or want to do.*

*I want to get you folks to Utah.*

*It is a good dream, I think. I think this land of yours very strange, though.*

*Why's that?*

*This police who comes to search here. He thinks he does the right thing, but the thing he does is not really right. You are doing the wrong thing by breaking the law, but breaking the law is the right thing to do.*

*Ours is now a world of extreme contradictions.*

*It is interesting.*

*Look, you're a bright girl. You should set your sights higher than being a hot actress married to a younger Tom Cruise. He's a dick, anyway.*

She laughs. *What sign of the zodiac is Mr. Sokolove?*

*Sokolove is Cancer.*

*The crab.*

We laugh about that too.


The law returns two days later. This time Miguel is on watch in the dark and sees them coming. In two minutes the whole family is huddling in the crawlspace beneath the rug under my desk in the office. Calloway's men rip the shit out of the place, slice the wallpaper in all the rooms wherever they touch a bump from an old glob of paint behind the paper, paint their high beam flashlights through the hidey hole in the office back room, search for trap doors in the utility room. They scrounge around the grounds. They look like raving lunatics dressed in the white gowns of a psychiatric ward, or maybe a religious cult. They don't know the family can actually access the spaces between walls from the crawlspace under my desk. They do extensive damage in the next two hours.

It's nearly 3:30 a.m. when they finish, the real witching hour when devils burst forth from the gates of Hell. I am reading the final chapter of *Lonesome Dove* at the office desk when a perspiring Calloway bursts in. I hold up a fresh bottle of water.

*Rest and Refreshment, Especially an Agent Calloway? You're perspiring like crazy. Our world must be getting hotter.*

*Bullshit it is. You can kiss my ass, Mister Schmidthead.* I don't let myself envision that, the kissing his ass. *People can't fuck up what God made.*

*God might be pretty busy, and he seems to be losing.*

*Fuck you. I will catch you.*

*Where is your humanity, Calloway? Why don't you find yourself a real job where you can contribute to the GDP like I have? Ever think maybe you in your government job suck off the nation's mammary more than illegals.*

*Illegals break the fucking law of the land, moron.*

*A really bad law in what is becoming a really bad land. It wouldn't be such a bad law if real people could really get in legally, but that's not really possible anymore. Doesn't seem real human.*

*I'm an agent first, human second.*

*Really.*

*You want them to suck up all the free shit citizens pay for? Like medical care?*

*I really don't care.*

*I do.*

*It's just organized crime sanctioned by government, anyway. Ultimate price-gouging.*

*Illegals are a people problem, a problem for all us people.*

*Illegals are people too.*

*Not American people. Isn't it obvious?*

*Sometimes when I write the word "obvious," I accidentally add an "L" and an "I" before the "V" as in "Liv." "Oblivious" instead of obvious, but that's just me. Come on, have a water. You've lost enough already with all that sweating, and all that effort looks like it put a strain on your heart, which I do think you really have.* I hold up the bottle. *Come on. Really. We all need water.*

He turns his back and walks right out the door. *Or not,* I say.


Right after he leaves is when Reyes rolls in with the new family—another mom and pop with many kidlets. Reyes looks like a rat, his stubble his feelers, a rat who loves digging. The family looks like a Mexican *Brady Bunch.* I set them up in four units. They get to crash and won't have to stand watches until Ximena's family leaves.

Which is nearly twenty-four hours later. Gamble calls and says pickup will be an hour before dawn. It will be sad to bid farewell to Ximena, but I know she is headed for a life better than mine. I don't know if Sokolove can survive her loss, though.

I find her standing alone outside with her water bottle and small backpack waiting for the rest of her family.

*You shouldn't be out here alone in the dark, Ximena. Coyotes. They travel in packs, and they're hungry these days.*

*I have seen them, Mister Smitty. They wear white shirts and sunglasses and drive big, black cars…*

*I will remember you when I see Pisces.*

*I will remember you when I see Aquarius. And who can forget the crab?*

We laugh a little.

*I hope you will see me in your visions, Mister Smitty. Maybe that's all we can ask for,* she says, *that we be remembered.* Too damn philosophical for such a young girl.

*I really wish I could remember more and not see so much.*

*I know.*

Her family joins us in the lot near Unit One when the headlights appear from Gamble's old box van a few miles out.

Sokolove sits in his wheelchair at his open door. Manuel and Guadalupe thank him profusely. My friend looks depressed.

They walk over to me. During their entire stay, I haven't heard more than a half dozen sentences from either of them. I guess they let their worldly daughter serve as their family ambassador. Manuel shakes my hand. *Gracias, senor. You are a very humane human being.*

*No worries. Deep down inside I truly suck. And I see things that aren't really there.*

*That is a gift.*

Ximena whispers to them. They listen and nod.

*We have gifts too,* he says. *Ximena says Mister Sokolove wants to see them.*

Sokolove perks up and nods vigorously.

Manuel then sings a song I have never heard. His voice dances up and down the scale. I am an educated man. I think. I probably attended college. Or wanted to. Whether I did or not, I know things, like the normal vocal range of a male voice oscillates between 85 and 180 hertz, but his encompasses the female range of 165 to 255 as well, and I think even lower and higher on the spectrum. It is a beautiful, other-worldly ballad. Then Guadalupe begins her dance. Every part of her body seems double-jointed, ankles, knees, wrists, thumbs, elbows, shoulders, even her hips. They pop in and out, forward and backward. She undulates like ebbing and flowing rivers. Her dance is art. As is his song. I don't think my brain is making this up on its own.

Sokolove hoots and hollers and claps. The singing and dancing subside.

Gamble rolls his van into the lot, gets out, and opens the rear doors. With his slicked back hair and bolo tie, he looks like a Vegas high roller.

The family moves toward him. Ximena lingers behind. She points to Sokolove's plant through his open door. *See, my sweet Gordito,* she says to him. *I brought it back from the dead. Gave it new life. Just like nursing a baby.*

He looks at it and nods. *No, shit,* he says. *You're an amazing wench.* Then he stares at his hands in his lap. My friend looks very sad.

*Que te la pique un pollo,* she says. I hope a chicken pecks at your dick.

*Yeah, well, go fry asparagus.* He waves her off.

She turns to me. *I was pulling your leg, Mister Smitty. Is that the expression? I don't really want to be an actress. I will be an environmental scientist. This world needs nursing back too, and my people need clean air and water. Yours too.*

*I think our people are the same,* I say.

*Maybe. I hope you are right.*

She touches my cheek, then whispers something into my ear. She blows Sokolove a kiss that flies through the air and enters his heart, where I hope it will live forever. Ximena then runs to the van and hops in. Gamble slams the rear doors, then gets in the driver's side and churns out of the lot.

I join Sokolove. *They were different,* I say.

*Yeah.*

*And Ximena … surprising.*

He smiles, his well-defined nasolabial folds cutting deeper into his face, as his eyes search the stars. *There are over eleven billion planets orbiting stars like ours, Smitty. We're not the only ones who fucked up their air and water. It's a big shitshow everywhere. Real people can't get into this airtight and watertight country unless we help them. We're doing a damn good thing.*

I am not shocked. *I guess people are the same just about everywhere, huh?*

*Yeah, carbon is carbon.* Then he laughs. *But some carbon can do the weirdest shit.*

*What about our regulars? Angel and Pena. Maria. Why didn't you tell me they are a family?*

*I was getting around to it.*

I then see each of them standing at their open doors. Pena's hands are twirling completely around slowly, first palms down, then up, then down again, rotating as if on axles. Angel is holding his quart bottle in his right hand down at his side, but his forefinger nonetheless stretches up to scratch his cheek. Maria's eyes are rolling horizontally in their sockets and changing color from desolate brown to emerald to ocean blue, then rolling vertically while changing colors just like a whirling slot machine.

*Damn!* I say. *Am I seeing this right?*

*Yeah. Just think of them as hall monitors in grammar school. Here to help when we need them.*

*And—*

*Reyes and Gamble are just good shits.*

He starts hacking terribly, and becomes a skeleton again. Now I know we really are near the end. *When I get to the next place,* he whispers, *I hope there is someone like you to let me in.*

I squeeze his hand. We both see the headlights from the two cars approaching miles out from the north, undoubtedly Ford Expeditions.

The new family scurries into the office.

I say, *I need to roll the desk back over the carpeted crawl space door.*

*What did she whisper to you?*

*Ximena? That Leenowlee means sweet, naïve man.*

*What else?*

*She's not really sixteen. She's … sort of sixteen.*

*I knew that. I'm going to miss that little wench. I wish I could see weird shit like you. Then maybe I could see her again.*

*I wish I could give you that gift before you leave me.*

*Tell me, what do you see out there right now?*

*I see them coming,* I say. *Coyotes.*

*No shit,* he says.

*No shit, and the coyote in charge has a penis head.*

# Sea Change
by Sara Ramey

There used to be a hermitage on Ispada's western promontory. The foundation stones are marooned on toothy
conglomerate, bare and dark where the low sandstone cliffs
have washed away. Seven years ago, my dad slowed the car
on the drive to the airport to look at the hermitage, still
standing then, though with a fatal lean.

"I wish someone had told me to remember what things
were like when I was a kid," he said.

Seven years, and my dad's right. The hermitage isn't
there anymore. The taxi's tires hush over a patch of unbro-
ken asphalt. I'm queasy, heavy with travel fatigue and the
insistent fear that nothing I loved about this place has en-
dured. The square window punched into the hermitage's
wall has collapsed, the roof rotted away, gone the click-
click-click of an endless drip, the sound refracting strangely
in the cloistered space. I was banned from playing there but
Lauren wasn't deterred by danger. She'd step through the
gap where a door used to be and look back at me, darkly
framed and waiting.

"Far out here, aren't you?" the cab driver says.

I've been giving him directions from memory for the past half hour. His GPS shows us driving over the ocean. Not many people on the coast think about Ispada, a bare-faced island big enough to be dangerous to ships at night but small enough to hide Maggie, who's been drowning sailors for centuries.

"Not that far," I say, but the driver is distracted, turning the radio dial when he isn't squinting at the cracked road. He's been fidgety since we left the mainland, perhaps sensing this island isn't part of the Washington he knows.

I was eighteen the last time I passed the crossroads where Lauren and I buried gifts for the Devil, because we'd heard that's where he likes to linger. We left out cookies for Santa, too. The problem was that we believed in everything. I'm in graduate school in Montana, but education hasn't changed what I'm willing to believe. It can't. I'm doomed to believe in childhood stories forever, because I know at least one that is true.

Half a mile from the hermitage and seated at the crest of a hill is Maggie's house, freshly whitewashed, shining, less gargantuan and secretive than it appeared to me as a kid. Farther down the road is my parents' house—yellow-brown and two stories perched on the hill's bald slope.

Between the houses is a diagonal crevasse where runoff carves a passage to the ocean. The coastal road floods in storms and water sweeps dangerously close to my parents' front porch. I used to dream our house was floating away, but that was one game Lauren wouldn't allow.

"This is it," I say when we come to my parents' gravel driveway. The driver shudders when he steps out to retrieve my suitcase from the trunk. His arms are goose bumped. I wish he'd take me to the front door, but I don't ask. He twists the scraggly end of his greying beard while I count out his tip.

He nods and gets back in the white-and-green cab. Brine and moist earth replace the cloying smell of his after-shave. A quarter mile down the road, he flips on his brights against Ispada's indistinct light. I feel less real in this light. Missoula is overcast and cold in mid-October but it's a Halloween cold, the cold before fires in the fireplace, or a groaning coil heater in a college dorm. Ispada's cold turns the air anemic. I remind myself I'm a native, but a sinking weakness creeps into my legs.

I yank the rolling suitcase up the depression at the bottom of the driveway. My dad hasn't filled in the potholes or planted decorative trees along the property like he said he would. He and my mom renovate their sailboat regularly—the newest nav system, the best water filtration—but it's harder to alter Ispada. The island resists improvement.

The town is visible to the east, clustered by the mouth of the two-lane bridge to Washington. After the fullness of Missoula's forests and mountains, the island appears naked except for a few outcroppings of stunted conifers and tufts of yellow brush, too frail to hold onto. Under the sandy top layers, the ground is brittle black stone. Lauren and I found a cave in the cliffs to the north. The cave wasn't large enough for an adult to enter but, at ten, I might have fit. Drafts of warm, rotting air breathed out from the shaft. Light snuck past my body, shivering over the algaed walls. Lauren wanted to call it the Wailing Abyss and use it in our games, but I refused to go near it after that first, deep look.

I hoist the suitcase over the last rough patch of earth and my tired body after.

A man stands up from a chair on the porch of my parents' house. I didn't see him at first. His shirt is green-brown flannel, camouflaged against the wall.

"Amelia?"

"Hello," I say. "Are you Henry?"

His dry lips crack on a smile. There's weight in his face, pulling down the corners of his eyes. He looks like he doesn't smile much.

"I thought the cab would take you up to the house," he says.

"Oh, it's okay. The suitcase rolls."

He reaches out for a handshake before taking my suitcase. He's built densely, with the stained work boots of a former fisherman, but his square fingernails are clean. A hint of musky cologne reaches me, unfamiliar and potent.

"I'll go in a minute," Henry says. "Your parents thought you'd want someone here to—"

"Make sure I arrive?"

"Welcome you."

My parents will be at sea for two more days. I waited until they were far down the Californian coast to tell them I'd be visiting over fall break. I suspected they'd ruin my first experience of home after seven years. I wanted things to feel the way they had when I was younger.

Henry opens the front door for me. When I don't step inside, he follows my eyes to Maggie's house.

"How is she?" I say.

Henry knows I'm a local but hesitates. I recognize the pause. It's ingrained in us on Ispada. Unlike with most of the things I was forbidden to do as a child, I never told outsiders about Maggie.

Maggie, when she visited my mom, was slim and tall, curved like a lily frond, sometimes draped in a sundress a few sizes too large or tight across the shoulders, like she didn't notice when clothes didn't fit. Maggie in her human form was nothing like the Disney mermaids I envisioned—coral shell bra, nacre smile, hair of undulating red kelp.

"She's slipping," Henry says.

My dad told me over the phone. Hushed, he said Maggie had met someone, a man who didn't fall for her lure. Sirens live forever until they meet someone who resists them. What comes after, no one knows. Henry's expression suggests it'd be painful to ask more.

He sets my suitcase down in the foyer and goes to the kitchen for a glass of water. After he hands it to me, he rambles. Opal, my parents' elderly cat, has plenty of food in the bowl. The thermostat is finicky, so if I need a fire in the fireplace, he can get one started, though he doesn't know when the chimney was last cleaned. His hands open and close on empty air, like he wishes he had something to grip. He's the kind of big man who doesn't know where to stash himself, so he hovers uncomfortably by the hallway table.

"Need anything, let me know," he says.

"Will you be at Maggie's?"

"Sometimes. I'm out a lot. Fixing up the place, running errands."

When I don't need anything more, he leaves. He looks relieved to go outside, where he can stand up straight without hitting his forehead.

I climb upstairs with my suitcase and exhaustion. My mom has filled my old room with boxes from when the real estate office was being remodeled. I recall her telling me this. Seeing it is different, surprising, though I couldn't have expected my parents to keep the room intact.

The floor is piled with junk from my dad's brief and discarded hobbies, though someone has cleared an aisle and made the bed. I don't mind sharing space with a pile of canvases and the smell of acrylics, stacks of yarn mounded into a bed for the cat, who glares out from beneath the overlarge wooden chair by the window.

I mean to stay awake and check my email, maybe work on my thesis, but the bed is impossible to resist and the comforter wraps itself around me.

It's dark when I open my eyes to the watery hush that used to be background noise, unnoticeable until a stranger pointed out the island's heartbeat. Damp seeps from the house, smelling of loam and soil. I sit up against the headboard, looking out the window at a light that seems to hover over the water.

I struggle out of the too-soft bed and stub my toes on the canvases. The pain clears some of the haze. A gibbous moon overhead makes it easier to see the jagged coast, though the sandstone steps Lauren and I used to follow are invisible. I find it hard, even hundreds of miles away in Montana, to convince myself that it's okay to leave buildings at night. Too many years of my dad telling me that I wasn't to go out—that it was safe, Maggie wouldn't harm someone living in her territory, but just in case, don't go out at night.

I had recurring nightmares of spider legs skritching at my door, wanting in. When I'm stressed, I dream of a presence in the dark.

I fumble to the bathroom and pull the chain for the light. The buzz overwhelms the house's small, shifting sounds. Opal's slitted eyes reflect light in the hall but she comes no closer. My mouth is fuzzy, a headache throbbing behind my eyes. I'm horse-faced with fatigue and my hair is a flat brown mat. I can't find a toothbrush under the sink, so I scrub my teeth with a finger and some paste from a rolled tube in the medicine cabinet.

The sense of loss I've learned to ignore is sharper here. I don't know if it's the threat of joblessness, guilt that I fall in and out of love within the week, or that I'd rather study folklore than volunteer and change the world and everything I'm supposed to want.

The boys on Ispada used to tease me for living so close to Maggie. Some of her strangeness rubbed off on me, they'd say when I pulled up a chair for Lauren, or set a plate for her at lunch.

Redheaded Benny, my first boyfriend, found me in college. That new, tender thing in the well of my chest didn't last after all the bars and social circles and gossip, a bombardment of noise I didn't care about. Then there was Malcolm, Mal, who moved in next door and fixed the screen on my window, and walked with me if I had to shop or attend class at night. I thought about, of all things, the arch of his black eyebrows. And as soon as his friends wanted to be my friends, the tender thing retreated into safe quietude. My studies never wavered, folklore my only sustainable love.

I wrap myself in the quilt and sit in the chair by the window until the wood warms to my body, the arms seeming to curve around me. I crave a decade here in the soft dark where thoughts can pass through me without sticking. The creak of the house like the living body of a ship. The air, stinging when I inhale, past the smell of drying paint. My fingertips find scars on the chair's worn finish, where, bored with homework, I pried up splinters with my pencil.

I wonder what it's like to be a siren, if wood feels like wood to Maggie. She's older than my grandpa could remember—as far as anyone knows, she's always lived on Ispada. Yet what we know about her fits in a whisper.

A bright flash draws my attention to the shore. I lean so close that my breath fogs the window.

He could've been anything—a late-night gull winging over the surf, a scrap of fabric caught on a driftwood spine. But no, the shape is human and solid. It must be Henry down by the water. He sways. He tilts and rights himself as the waves cast hooks into his body and tug.

He catches himself and stumbles away from the surf. The door to Maggie's house opens. Unearthly light spills out, welcoming, like the arms of the chair.

Of course, I think. Henry lives there.

*

I remember Maggie in a lavender sundress. She sat on the settee in my parents' living room. Her head turned, as if she felt my gaze on her, and her seal eyes were black and unending.

My mom dropped her knitting into her lap when she saw me in the doorway. "Amelia, we're busy," she said.

Maggie's smile was crooked, unpracticed. "Not at all. Merely visiting."

"Sorry," I said. I slipped my backpack from my shoulders. "School got out early. The whole hallway's flooded. I guess a pipe burst or something."

The school is three classrooms, offices, and a lunchroom with shelves for the library. There were six people in my grade.

"Won't you join us?" Maggie said. I couldn't remember her ever addressing me directly. She had lunch every other Friday with my mom, who knitted while they talked. The old families in town took turns hosting Maggie.

"No, that's okay," my mom said. "You want to get back to your games."

"Mom, I'm sixteen. Are you okay?"

I'd never seen her that way, flushed and fumbling the knitting needles. There was a ragged hole in the few lines she'd managed but she didn't seem to notice.

That's it, I thought of Maggie's luminous skin and a hum I could feel but couldn't track. That's the lure.

My parents had rules about Maggie. I wasn't to be alone with her. I couldn't sass Maggie even when I was tired or hungry. The special treatment gave her a mysterious air that lent itself well to games of make-believe. My knowledge of her as a siren came gradually, and Lauren and I filled the gaps in our understanding with imagination. Maggie became a witch who cursed us or Nimue, the Lady of the Lake, who entrusted us with a sacred task. When we were old enough to know her as a siren, Lauren was disappointed because Maggie could only ever be just that one thing.

The house is chilly when I get up and everything, the flush of the toilet and the squeak of the ungreased doorknob, is unbearably loud. It's sunny but not the boisterous sunniness of a Montana day. The light of Ispada is numb with cold.

I dress and walk up the road to Maggie's house, the distance shorter than it used to feel. Henry has installed new supports for the sagging roof and cleared weeds from the foundation. Lauren once wanted me to crawl behind the latticework under the porch.

"Come on, you baby," she said. "Pretend it's the belly of a worm. Let's see what it's eaten."

The problem was I believed too readily. Lauren was the one who knew what was real and what wasn't. As long as she had home and our parents, she could wander anywhere and have a place to return to that never changed. She didn't like my dream that the house floated away because how could she come home if home wasn't anchored to the earth?

My calves burn as I crest Maggie's hill. From up here, the ocean is a shifting backdrop.

Maggie walks out the front door as I approach, as if she were waiting for me. A shiver works up my spine at the sight of her perfectly oval face and those deep-set eyes.

"I heard you needed to get away, darling." The click of her tongue makes *darling* sound like *darkling*.

"Maggie," I say and stop. I sound dull after her whiskey, telemarketer voice.

She steps close to wrap a hand around my elbow. I can feel her sharp bones through my jacket.

146

"Amelia," she says. "I have not seen you in—how long has it been? Years? Your mother told me you would be visiting. Come inside. I have tea ready."

I feel groggy after sleeping for so long but my name on her tongue shocks me alert.

In her kitchen, we sit on stools at the marble counter, a new addition, and Maggie pours us tea in ceramic mugs rimmed blue with cartoon waves. I peel off my jacket and drape it over a rung of the stool.

Lauren dared me to peer through the window of Maggie's house. The curtains were tatters and the vaulted rooms cobwebbed. There was one set of footprints in the layer of dust on the floor, as if Maggie stepped carefully in her own tracks when she walked to the back door.

Now pans hang overhead, and the splintering floor is replaced with sanded hardwood—all of it new, as is the fit of Maggie's white silk blouse, delicately collared, with turquoise buttons.

"It's Darjeeling," she says and smiles.

I inhale the steam rising from my mug. "Thank you. The house looks nice. And you, I mean, your clothes. You look nice."

Maggie's smile is steady, her eyes too intense to be happy. Her face is sprinkled with tiny scales. I decide I imagined them when they disappear a moment later and her skin is smooth.

"Henry is teaching me a lot about the world," Maggie says. She pushes toward me a plate of glazed scones, studded with cranberries. "Have one, please. Henry picked them up this morning."

"I didn't hear a car," I say. I slept so deeply this shouldn't be a surprise, but I used to wake up if anyone drove down the road.

"Henry likes to walk to town," she says. "We have that in common."

I take a scone to be polite but as soon as I see it on my napkin, I have to take a bite, then another, suddenly ravenous. Maggie sips her tea while I devour a second.

The scales reappear, faint on the swan's curve of Maggie's neck. I'm not imagining them, but they disappear as soon as my eyes fix on the spot. We're motionless long enough for me to realize how quiet it is, how posed we are at our breakfast tea, before the ocean sounds again and Maggie tips her chin down to her mug. I feel—not hunted, but observed.

"How is your college?" she says.

"I'm in graduate school, my last year."

"My apologies. I forget things so easily these days. It is good that I have Henry here to remind me. He is all the audience I need."

"You mean—" I stop myself, but she intuits my question anyway.

"He is my prey?" She laughs. Her small sounds are toneless. No, they're all the same spectral tone, only rhythm to distinguish them. "Henry is different. He refuses to be mine entirely, though he could be, if he chose. The death of a daughter is reason enough, is it not, darling?"

There it is again. Darkling.

"His daughter died? That's terrible."

"Enough about us," she says abruptly. Her hand, surprisingly leathery, closes over mine. "I want to know about you."

I wonder if my dad told her I study folklore, which I hope Maggie doesn't understand as an obsession with her. I can't tell if she's trying to scare me or if she's always been this way, so keen, with an edge of mockery. We've never had a conversation by ourselves before, but the setup—my parents sailing, Maggie alone in her whitewashed house—suddenly feels precarious.

Her lips are wildflower pink and when she looks down at our hands, her eyes are lightless. "Perhaps you could tell me about your work."

"My work." I free my hand and wrap it around the mug. "Did my mom tell you I'm getting my master's? Comparative literature."

Her head tilts. "Comparative?"

"I study how different cultures recycle folklore."

"You study stories?"

"Yes."

"And this is the work of your life?"

From anyone else, the question would be derisive.

"Yeah, it is. Maybe too much," I say. She looks questioning and I try to smile. "I had some chances to get to know people and didn't."

"Lovers?"

"Boyfriends. Benny was back in college but Mal and I broke up a few months ago. He's a grad student too, in psychology."

"An inquiry into himself, perhaps." Maggie refills our mugs. I imagine her eyes turn silver, but that's the light glinting off the pans hanging overhead, blinding me.

Mal knocked on my apartment door the day I moved in, about to start grad school. He held out a cheap bottle of wine and a bag of Fritos. "The stipends are terrible," he said, "but the company's alright."

"Did you love him?" Maggie says.

"Love him? I didn't know him."

"That is not a requirement for love. Henry will tell you." Her voice is cautious, or maybe bitter. The siren swims under her face, an expression more than anything, as remote as deep water.

Maggie notices my shiver and pulls a shawl from the hall closet to wrap around my shoulders. I look out the bay windows, which face west toward the ocean. There's a birch in back, weighted with what I think are black leaves until one twitches and an entire branch lifts into the air, a swirling flock of starlings.

Maggie claps her palms over her ears. "Do they have to be so loud?"

Henry passes under the tree with gloves and a toolkit. The birds quiet. When he's gone, the starlings land again, strong feet stripping the white bark.

"It's brave of him," Maggie says, unsmiling.

"What is?"

"Being my companion."

I tug the shawl tight around me. "How did it happen?"

Scales spread across the exposed slope of her collarbone, up the column of her throat. "He was out, fishing, and heard my call. He desired escape, or he would not have answered, but when I offered him truth and forgetting, he sang a lullaby I had nearly forgotten."

She hums. The sound darts through me. Scales surface on the skin beneath her darkening eyes and I remember Henry saying she's losing control.

The back door creaks.

"Maggie?" Henry steps inside. He stands between me and Maggie so that all I can see is the quilted back of his jacket.

"It's okay," I say. "I'm alright."

Henry lingers nearby, pretending to knot twine while we wash the dishes. Maggie's edges dull. She works methodically but slowly, passing me mugs to dry. I feel safe with Henry there. The question I circle time and again is impossible to resist, knowing soon Maggie will be as human as I am.

"What's it like to be a siren?" I say.

I feel Henry look up. Maggie brushes my cheek with her sudsy fingers. I feel her lure hooked on my ribs, tugging when her attention narrows in on me. Nothing matters under her hazy regard except the two of us.

"We love fully, once a year," she says, "and never any other time. But there are many, many years. A long life is a gift if you know how to forget." She withdraws her hand but water drips down my face like she's still touching me.

She curls up on a window seat in the lofted living room, seeming to forget that we're here. Her bare feet arch over the hardwood floor. I am short and dark compared to her.

Henry gestures for me to follow him out. The door shuts behind us, and I wish I had my jacket. The yarn of the shawl smells faintly of brine and musk. The scent that clings to Henry—it must belong to Maggie.

The birds freeze when we step out but start up again when we walk to the corner of the wraparound porch. The rocks below are overgrown with hardy salt-bitten lichen but Henry has scraped clean the posts holding up the awning. Farther out is the promontory, remnants of the hermitage in stone piles like cairns.

Some of the women in town used to take turns bringing Maggie supplies every Sunday after church. Lauren and I would watch that week's delivery arrive, a box set down by the front door, with a disposable casserole dish on top.

"We have to remind her not to hunt among us," my mom said.

Maggie can't have missed their fearful obligation. Perhaps it pleases her. No one from Ispada ever followed her lure, but neither did they tend to her the way Henry does.

Henry's cheeks sag under girlish lashes. He must be in his fifties. It occurs to me that I don't know why he stays with Maggie—if he's compelled by the lure, or if he wants to be with her. They must have sex. Her smell is on him, burgeoning and moist.

I glance behind us at the bay windows, glazed with light.

"It's the lure," Henry says. "We're all drawn to her."

"I forgot what it feels like. I'm afraid," I say, half to myself.

Henry shakes his head. "I won't say not to be. But the call isn't what you think, not exactly. It gives you a choice."

"What choice?"

"You can't understand. You're only feeling the edge of it, but in the middle—" He puts his hand on his chest as if to check that he's here. "No one chooses to stay."

"You stayed."

"She needed me to stay. How long before someone figures her out? This isn't a world for creatures like her anymore. And I like her, without—the rest of it." The rest of her, he should have said.

Maggie comes out to stand by the rail and looks at us as if through a dark pane.

"She's really turning human?" I say, low, though I'm not sure she can't hear.

"More and more," Henry says. "She feels the siren dying. She's afraid, too."

He puts a clumsy hand on my shoulder and crosses the porch to stand beside Maggie but doesn't touch her. Her eyes are for the ocean and his eyes are for her. He looks at her as if she's the brightest light he can stand. He leans in, grazing her hand with his work-toughened fingers, those clean square nails. She turns to him incrementally, sweeps him with a glance softened by closeness. He's so earthy, so human next to her, but she isn't unmoved. I don't know where Maggie ends and the siren begins.

Everything I know about sirens seems inadequate when I see Maggie and Henry side by side. The siren peers out of her eyes, the pupils too large. Maybe it's the indirect light, but Maggie seems older than she used to be. There are shadows on her face that I haven't seen before.

*

Back at my parents' house, I search for cell service and answer a tepid email from my advisor, who's too busy with work of her own to hound me about mine.

I open a window and lean out to call my parents on the satellite phone.

"Amelia," my mom says, her voice muffled by a rasping wind. "Can you hold on a minute?"

"Sure." I rest my elbows on the sill. Inside, the air of my old room is cluttered. There's the dresser I carved my initials on with a kitchen knife. The blue comforter I inherited from my grandma covers the bed. After dinner, when it was too dark to play outside, Lauren and I would throw the quilt over some kitchen chairs to create the Cave of Untold Doom, where innumerable stuffed animals and dolls needed rescuing from underwater caverns.

I imagined Lauren as taller and two years older than me but with the same black hair that frizzes in humidity. She was first through the door, first to come up with a new way to make the isolation bearable.

"Amelia?"

"I'm here."

"Hi, sorry." My mom's voice is stronger. "I had to find a place out of the wind. You made it to the house alright?"

"Yeah. It's less fun without you guys here, but one more day, right?" I peel up the flap of a box stacked by the window. The files inside are coffee stained, unwanted. "I saw Maggie today and met Henry."

"What'd you think? She's getting weirder, right?"

I remember her shifting scales and moments of uncertainty. "She's turning human. That has to be strange for her. I think her hearing's changing. I bet people will be happy when the lure's gone for good."

I don't know what she reads in my voice, but she says, "You sure you're alright?"

"Yeah," I say. "Just missing things. Everything's different enough that it feels off."

"That sounds like growing up," my mom says and laughs. "I'll make you cocoa with peanut butter when we get in."

After we hang up, I try to finish the edits my advisor suggested but my thoughts are blurry. I heat up a frozen dinner and eat it in slow bites over my laptop keyboard. Time slurs, purposeless.

I go up to my room to sit in the chair. Beyond the branches of the trees out back, the stars are crisp. An itch travels up my legs and the ocean rolls darkly on the near shore, each wave like a crook of her finger.

Come nearer, the water says. Come roll in the cold bath. I will hold you.

I spot Henry by the shore, looking out like a fishwife waiting for her husband to sail home.

I watch until he walks back to Maggie's house, then I get up to wash my face in the bathroom. My bangs hang limply across my forehead. I look wan, empty. When I go back to my room, the cat has taken my seat by the window. I sift through the ache of memory and sink into bed, wondering if this is what it feels like to be haunted.

*

The next day, I'm typing out citations in the living room when I see Maggie out the window. She walks as if asleep and her gaze skips over me. Henry watches from her house. I hike up to meet him, glancing back to check Maggie's progress until she disappears beyond the swell of a hill. Henry pours me breakfast tea and sets out a plate of bakery banana bread. We eat it with cream cheese at Maggie's new kitchen table, that has chairs enough for six but never people to fill them. We pretend we aren't watching the door, waiting for her to return.

"She gets like this," he says.

Maggie has been welcoming but something crawls under her face when I look at her from the corner of my eye. My hair stands up when it happens. I remember staring into the cliffside cave, hearing the echo of unseen water.

Maggie comes back by the time we're done eating but shakes her head when I say hello.

"They're never quiet," she says, hands over her ears.

Henry opens the closet, pulls out a pellet gun, and walks out the back. I watch through the bay window as he raises the gun. I jerk when the first shot cracks, dropping a black-feathered body. The starlings scatter from the bare branches, screaming. Crack. Another starling crumples. He shoots again but the birds fly out of range.

I feel sick and leave before Henry comes back inside. I sit by an open window in my parents' living room until the battery dies in my phone, and eat a granola bar from the pantry, imagining my parents anchored off some stretch of coastline, maybe curled up in their bunk below deck.

The daylight is gone before I notice it's fading.

When Henry appears, I pull on boots and walk down to the shore, tripping over stones in the dark. I stop a few feet away and look up at his silhouette.

He's different under the moon. The sag of his cheeks, the wrinkles—marks of time dissolve. He looks as if he has always stood on this shore.

Silver-skimmed crests tumble over the pebbles at our feet. The ocean is a maw, rocks its teeth and water the spit rolling in its mouth. I shiver and wrap my arms around my stomach, over my coat. Mist falls over us from waves hitting rocks on the shore.

Henry's lips move. I follow his gaze to the roiling ocean, turning over at our feet. The wash of the foam across the pebble-studded ground is mesmerizing. The moon is full enough that I can see tiny air bubbles rise from the wet sand. A tangle of seaweed catches on my boot. I don't have to imagine what Henry sees in the waves. As I watch them shift and beckon, I feel how right it is that we wait for her.

A pale form rises from a deeper part of the water. Its features are smoothed over with opalescent scales, the suggestion of a nose and lips and eye sockets beneath, the hair stringy and grey but long, down to feminine hips. The hum in the back of my mind crests, a relentless rhythm. I grip a fistful of my shirt and hold onto myself.

Henry leans toward her and back with the ebb of the surf.

He steps forward but doesn't enter the water, though it murmurs ceaselessly. The siren sheds light, softening the surface of the impenetrable waves.

The creature's hand rises. The light gentles and her skin takes on a pink and delicate cast.

She's lovely and more familiar to me than my own face. I want to wrap myself around her, let her carry us into the savage heavy place. In the slick of moisture on her ghastly skin, I see the comfort of the ocean's depth, the velvet bed waiting for me at the bottom. She will unwrap me, and then she will let me rest.

Henry, too, shakes with violent longing. His voice is a growl at first, easily ignored. But it makes the siren turn her eyes from me. The weaker her song, the stronger Henry's becomes. He sings about a fishing boat with peeling paint and a net he lost to a frayed knot, banal human things that promise an aching back, but also another day.

The siren's hand falls. Her light dims. All that loveliness withers and the black ocean drips from her balding skull. Ragged fingernails curl against her thighs and her wrinkled breasts sag against the concave chest, fleshless skin stretched over an alien canvas, her features indistinct in the eyeless mask of a face.

She slumps, boneless, back under the waves.

Henry staggers out of the water. He falls back on the sand with me and heaves, and neither of us speaks for a long time.

When I can breathe again, I say, "Why? Why did you sing? Didn't you feel her?"

Sand clings to his beard. He meets my eyes. His voice is hoarse and aged, as if the siren whittled down all but this sliver of him.

"I feel her. She's not as strong as she used to be."

I push up on my elbows. It's harder than it should be. "Why didn't you let me go?"

The lines in his face return. His eyes have borrowed some of Maggie's darkness when he looks at me across the salted earth.

"She makes the bottom of the ocean feel lovely, doesn't she? But all it is, is death, and Maggie's worth staying for." His lips stretch and bare his teeth. I almost don't recognize love. "I'll see her again when I'm done here."

I'll see her again—he isn't talking about Maggie. I know he must have felt the promise of reunion with his daughter in the siren's light.

He gave up what I've been circling for twenty-five years. I want to hate him for changing Maggie, but only by staying away forever could I have believed nothing was different on Ispada. Pretending is harder as my recollections of Lauren grow distant. The wound of her nonexistence aches. I miss loving someone so entirely that everyone else is a frail imitation. Will there ever be room in me for more?

The water washes up and fills my boots, cold now that the lure is a memory of itself, a call so faint I'm not sure if it's real or imaginary.

# Madrina
by Sara Rivera

### Part I: Godmother
*16 October 3011*

That night she woke in water, and it was daytime. Late afternoon, she would guess. She was floating on her back, looking up at a reddening sun and cliffs lost under heaps of green. The wide, backlit glisten of a waterfall gashed out between leaf and rock, fractured into smaller falls. She couldn't see rainbows but imagined they parted white mist all around her.

The water that cradled her felt warm, thick, lotioned. She looked down and saw that the water was green, the grey green of a smoked emerald, a water tone she'd never seen before.

As far as she could tell, she was alone, alone with sun and cliff and this body, this new body. She examined it. Underwater, she ran her fingers over her new stomach, small but very round. The arms and legs were soft too. Her skin was dusky brown like a fig. The seam of a white shirt curled around the tops of her ribs and its light fabric billowed in the water, a cloud around her chest.

Beautiful. Divine. Where was she? She didn't care.

It always took a moment—sometimes up to an hour—for the *madrina's* memories to enter her mind after knocking around at the periphery like tentative guests. Today, the first thing to bubble up was a word: *skydclan*. It meant family, or something like family. The madrina was lying in the water alone to avoid her skydclan, whoever they were. They were all gathered somewhere in a stone house in ambient light, celebrating, and she was expected there, expected to stand like a pillar in the center of a hive of children. The madrina wasn't avoiding the celebration out of malice or boredom. She was relishing a moment of privacy.

Body in water. Water on skin. No one else here. It had been months since the madrina had last seen this place empty. Maybe because summer was ending, and though the water retained warmth the air above felt like it had been blown off the height of a mountain. People stayed inside unless, like tonight, they went out to celebrate a feast day. Tonight they would light lanterns and float them downriver. Pinpoint lights like fireflies, LEDs. The madrina would meet her children, she decided, on their way to the river. She had time. She could rest a bit longer.

The visitor in the madrina's body had almost forgotten that she had a purpose. But how could she force herself to inventory every detail of their surroundings when all her madrina wanted was to close her eyes and rest? Silt shifted, clay-slime beneath their back. The sun descended incrementally. Now it crowned the shadow-green.

"I'm in a warm spring," the visitor said out loud, testing the madrina's voice.

Saying things out loud had always helped her. That, and she always delighted in the sound of a new voice, its musculature and music. Every voice felt different from first vibration to final projection. This voice made her grin. So high, almost girl-like, and yet silver swirls of hair ferned out in the water. This woman was young and not young at once.

"That sounds right," said the madrina. "I still feel like if I wanted to do a flip, I could."

The visitor started. Water rippled away. It happened, sometimes, with a powerful personality. The madrina would speak too, using their joint voice, and it felt like talking to yourself but not knowing what your self was going to say. The visitor had experienced three such conversations before. The technology was designed to incite certain emotions: instead of fighting an invader, the madrina welcomed a visitor, and shared a story.

"What are the children celebrating?" asked the visitor.

"It's the festival of Halflight," said the madrina. "Our solstice. That's what you used to call it, mm? Or Samhain? Mmm. Isn't the water warm? I thought I'd be alone but here you are."

*Time stamp: knowledge of the words solstice, Samhain. Places them in the past.*

"I like being alone with you," said the visitor.

"Aren't you nice. You're like a relative, but not so looooud."

A twist of laughter in their mutual mouth. The madrina and visitor at once raised wet fingers to their lips and smeared water across them, moistening. It was unclear who directed the action.

"It's almost time for me to go," said the madrina. "The sun's almost gone." Shadow had fallen across the water, tumbled rock and tree.

"It's almost time for me to go too," said the visitor. "But I want to stay."

"This is your house too. Come back someday."

"What's your name?" asked the visitor.

"Avila."

"Lilet. I have this feeling, Avila. It's like I just adore you."

Avila laughed, and Lilet felt some pity in that laughter. She felt it deep in their mutual belly.

## Part II: Trigger

*The M.A.D.R.I.N.A Project Casebooks: Mimicry Anthropology through Direct Reallocation and Intertemporal-Substitution by Neural Affinity*

Verbal Agreement 00:15 - 00:31 - 30 October 3011
Entry by Lilet DeEsparza, Ph.D

*This is a free-flow journal entry requested by Dr. Nadya Shiburo. I've been asked to read aloud a transcript of a diary entry following the 13 MAY TRIGGER EVENT. MADRINA archives require documentation to account for the quick and full reinstation of our funding. I have stated for the record that my journals are personal rather than analytic in tone, so this account is recommended for grouping with other data of its kind concerning the TRIGGER EVENT.*

# Begin

*When it began, the labs looked like they were sleeping. Bugs floated all viscous. People were quiet. The Bailey was turned off: safing, and dark. Safe mode never makes you feel safe.*

*Our Ayelids stayed on. As we walked around, we saw double dark: what was in front of us, and the eyelid overlay that narrated what was happening, what safe mode meant, the classification of the trigger event. One level above error: very mild.*

*It had been a couple years since the last trigger, long enough to make peace with it. Now here we all were, skirting corners, talking in whispers like rats, cradling our rats as if they were pets, laughing out of turn, lecturing ourselves and each other, anything, I think, to suppress that tiny part of ourselves that thought we might die, could die, would die, suspended and vacuumed in space. One night, the whole ship heaved, and we fell back against the walls. The ship made that awful breathing sound that it makes when we jump—only we couldn't be jumping.*

*A vision of our bodies blinking out. Our hearts clenched into nothing by cold. Those images you construct for yourself are powerful. Also, you grow up having to study them on the Bailey.*

*When the lights came back on it took us a few days to trust them. When everything began to hum and click and zoom around us like normal, we felt we should no longer be terrified. But we were. We didn't know what had happened. CC hadn't given the all-clear. In fact, for two days, they* didn't say anything. The news stream on Ayelid reiterated old information.

Normal life on the Bailey was undercut then by a climate of secrecy. People (nanotech experts, communications experts) started getting called in to CC, one by one, and they'd come out looking so old and tired. If any of them broke that silence, I didn't hear about it.

Eventually they had to tell us. Each sector in turn: an attempt to contain and control the spread of panic. Mine was third.

We were gathered in the starfield room. They did this on purpose because no one could hear us, and only CC could let us out, and they wouldn't, not right away, not in the heat of it.

I remember only a few words of Captain Ruiz's monologue, the ones that became a refrain in my mind for the next month:

We are lost.

We've lost communication with Earth.

We've lost communication with Katla.

We experienced a safe mode malfunction that resulted in an accidental jump. CC tech was affected. If any believe they can help, we are assembling a team of specialists to continue researching, to determine our location, to come up with options. In the meantime, full ongoing project research allocation for this sector goes to the location-stamp technology of the MADRINA project, in case consciousness travel can give us the location of Earth.

I repeat: we've lost communication with Katla.

We've lost communication with Earth.

We don't know where we are.

*It took only a minute for our audience to become a mob vibrating with its own anger and stress. The more passive people like me just went numb.*

*In the days to come, panic would ripple. It would generate grief cycles. You came out of that cycle determined to just work because you weren't dead yet, and every now and then, when you saw the brilliant minds who were working together threads of hope would ignite in you. How could humanity not find a solution? Someone would look out the window, find the right clue, and find out where we were. Of course they would.*

*Sure enough, people outside of the task force started making an avalanche of beamcoms to CC. I recognize the star system! I know where we are! But they were wrong every time.*

*After awhile, CC didn't even bother to say anything. They went quiet. That quiet sliced and gored us. We didn't know what to do with so much uncertainty. We still don't.*

End

## Part III: Midnight
### 16 October 3011

Lilet's lips had started to go blue inside the chamber, so they pulled her out.

The air that greeted her felt like it came out of a tin can. The light that greeted her had been set to *sunset* and the liquid she woke in felt like cold mucous. The first thing she did was scratch her left arm. That was the only thing she knew for sure: her arm itched. Otherwise, she couldn't name anything in the room. Nothing in focus, not even the familiar text overlay from her Ayelid. It danced in her unfocused vision.

She started thrashing. She thrashed toward the light and a hundred pinpricks of pain rippled across her body as the TimeWires were torn out. Two sets of arms caught her, restrained her, and tried to extract the wires correctly.

By the time her own memories returned—not tepidly knocking at the door, but slammed back into from different angles—she was out of the TimePool, dripping on the composite floor. The arms that held her upright belonged to Nadya and Dabo, project head and chemist. Nadya's arms held her forcefully, Dabo's tenderly.

Dabo was removing the remaining wire from her forearms and clotting spots of blood with a cotton ball. When she saw him, and knew him, her body and breath gradually stilled.

"You look familiar," Lilet said.

"Once I went to nice restaurant on East Plankta Promenade," he said. "They served us prickly pear preserves. Bright green, globby, and lots of seeds."

"Is that what I look like right now?" she said, her voice weak but smiling.

"That's what you look like right now," Dabo said.

It was an old game of theirs. She'd tell him he looked like something normal, or bland, and he'd tell her she looked like something creative, specific, grotesque, because he knew that she loved the grotesque.

She eased her elbows away: she could stand on her own. She looked past Dabo at the TimePool, which the interns were already mopping, one of them gathering loose wires into her arms like a little silver bird's nest.

*

A week after the Time Pool incident, Dabo came to visit her in bed. Lilet could've transferred to her own bed, to theirs, at any point, but she *liked* this station bed. Bailey scientists and engineers had gotten good at creating basic materials from nothing, or close to nothing. Lilet slept in on one of their printed mattresses. Every point and angle of her body that made contact with the mattress hummed with satisfaction.

Or maybe she only told herself she was satisfied. She tried to convince herself that she liked being so immobile. She didn't talk to herself about the longing that had shattered across her heart since meeting Avila, about the strange sadness that choked her. It too touched every point of her body, sinking her deeper.

That week, Lilet mostly stayed in bed even though her hips groaned. She simply couldn't convince herself wake up.

"Hi, corazón," Dabo said as he sat beside her one morning, greeting her in the language her mother had spoken. They always greeted each other this way. A tether to Earth and self.

"Titili," she said. Greeting the language his mother had spoken.

She looked down as he took her hand. It was the first time she realized that the colors she'd loved so much in Avila's world were the colors of their skin: hers a smoked emerald, a cold, rich green, Dabo's a deep forest black. A side effect of being born and raised on the Bailey.

"Say the word," he said. "And I turn this whole room into a game of pinball."

She laughed.

"You want to tell me about it today?" he asked.

"You've got study voice on," she said. "Like you can't help it."

"Ayla is very worried about you."

"Soffing named your Ayelid."

"I want to help."

There it came again: the shadow. Like the room of her mind had been set to *midnight.*

"Let me sleep, my butterfly," she said.

*

Verbal Agreement 00:00 - 00:24 - 26 October 3011
Entry by Lilet DeEsparza, Ph.D

*My name is Dr. Lilet DeEsparza. I am a participant in the MADRINA Project and this documentation pertains to a targeted TimePool study that took place October 16th, 3011, at 22:00 BAILEY TIME. Researchers are asked to bear in mind the parameters of the study, which equates neural flux following consciousness-travel to the condition of sleep paralysis. This is my seventh TimePool trial. My personality type is INTP.*

*I remember a warm spring at the bottom of a waterfall. Type: 1067 A. Host was alone in the spring. Clothed. Garment type: Split, 24 X7, wait. Maybe she wasn't wearing— never mind. Skin palette: tumbleweed, oatgrass, midnight. Hair type: star streak, lemongrass. Language stamp: Nordic. My best time stamp: mid-23rd century. The host placed Samhain and LED lighting in the past. Society: agrarian.*

*Unusually green. Request to compare against other TimePool data in NORDIC countries as my specialty is LATINAMERICA.*

*If I were to describe my waking experience along the color chart, I'd say that over the span of the past week I've felt turquoise and navy. I'm aware that this is not typical of my assessments following a TimePool shift, but is consistent with previous terminated participants. I feel like someone has died.*

## Part IV: Anthropology
### 4 June 3015

Verbal Agreement 00:00 - 00:13 - 4 June 3015
Entrev. Coady Ka-Vera, Katla MCOMM, c/ Lilet DeEsparza, Ph.D

*INT: What does it mean to you to be here? To have set foot on land?*

DES: It's almost … waking up, there's morning. And I've known mornings through TimeWire but it's very different to experience morning every day. You almost have too many options. The other day I went onto the Bailey and didn't leave until it was *spurod* out because I get overwhelmed by how many different places I could go. I think the human body and mind has only so much ability to internalize new sensory information. So I spend some time out, some time in…

I don't mean to diminish it. It means everything. It's land. For the first time I'm anchored to place. I'm just trying to express that it's as terrifying as it is euphoric.

*Spurod?*

Oh sorry. That means space-dark. Dark inside as outside, if you're in space.

*I understand. My parents grew up on Noptera, the first ship, and talked me a lot about their first year on Katla. It's longer than an Earth year, so you know, they had to get used to cycles.*

That's what it is, cycles. Onboard the Bailey all we could do was mimic cyclical time. We were prepared, I guess, as much as we could be—obviously, there were so many medical professionals onboard, everywhere you turned there was another doctor speculating and publishing on what our bodies would do the second we were exposed to Katla. They prepared us for the fact that we'd probably be sick a lot, especially those of us raised on the ship, even with the precautionary treatments. We had never been exposed to changing weather. I've felt sick most of the time since I've arrived and have been badly sick about four times now.

*Since you mention doctors, something I was going to ask: things were structured a little differently on the Bailey because it was designed to service that transition from Earth to Katla. Nadya told me that you didn't really choose your professions. Can you tell me about that?*

Honestly it was what I knew. It didn't feel rigid. Maybe it did for other kids. There was room on the Bailey for occupations outside of science, they just weren't the preference and there weren't many people available who could offer a high degree of training in those fields. And basically our operational web was a snapshot of what was live and available at the time we left Earth. So people could learn how to do things, how to play music, I guess. It was outdated information but the up-to-date information from Earth wasn't relevant to us anyway. Not aboard the Bailey, and not here on Katla. Once we got here, the only immediate reality had to be this one.

But cultural anthropology, my field, I got into it because I liked behavior. I liked biology too and anthropology became this synthesis of mind and body. For a long time though I actually thought I'd go into entomology because as a kid I *loved* bugs. I loved massive holos, filling my whole room with the insects of the Amazon and I'd play insects with my brother, tell him to pretend to be a helicopter damesfly. He'd try to act like that insect. At some point, I became more interested in the boy imitating the damselfly than the damselfly itself. I wanted to know why we do what we do. The educators aboard the Bailey were attuned to that shift.

*And how did you get involved, then, in the MADRINA project?*

It was initially a collaboration. The MADRINA collaborative grew out of the development of TimeWire, because it was important to the initial developers of TimeWire to keep consciousness travel ethical. It's an invasive technology, but also a technology that with an extraordinary potential to change the narrative of the past, to give us insight into the past, particularly the undocumented past, which we determined, in the western colonial societies we were interested in, meant the matrilineal past.

*When I first heard about this, I admit that I was hesitant. Isn't entering the mind of someone just another act of colonization? Someone other than the madrina is ultimately going to be writing her story.*

It's a difficult ethical question. You're putting a lot of power in subjective hands. And I can't speak for the original collective or the entirety of their dialogue, but for me, as a participant and ultimately as a consciousness traveler ... each trip was about listening. Honestly, when you go back, you don't have a lot of time, or it takes so much time to get your bearings that you're not going to bring back a revisionist history. You'd need a lot more information to really place that person's story in the constructs of their society. All you have time for is an impression. And, if you're lucky, a conversation. You get to know people in the past. People who are not known today, who were otherwise forgotten. It's like you're filling in a blank on this larger map of humanity. Maybe you're filling it in with something hazy and insubstantial, but at least it isn't blank anymore.

*Why women?*

The original collective was all women, born or identified. And yes. They were interested in women's stories and reconfiguring the world as matrilineal. But it was also that consciousness travelers match to women 8 times out of 10. It's unclear how that matching happens. It seems to vary depending on how strictly gender roles were enforced or embedded in a certain culture at a certain time and how those roles were tied to biological sex. I've shared consciousness with a transwoman living in 2018, but I know people who have shared transgender consciousness in cultures and time periods when there was no societal language with which to identify what that meant. Which was fascinating. It meant that the MADRINA project could go beyond what the madrinas themselves were allowed, culturally, to be aware of or. The point is to say that with MADRI-

NA, we focused on women's stories, but "woman" means many things and we're still learning, across the entirety of history and time, what all the meanings are.

## Part V: Dwooning
*27 October 3011*

Lilet walked down the hall in tinned darkness. All light was soft, peripheral, humming, beeping. An off-green glow from a lab to her left. An intermittent red alarm light to her right. All around her, rectangular space: the familiar blue-grey framework of the Bailey. Her Bailey. Her halls, the only ones she'd known.

Her station bed was located within the secure TimeWire zone. Her security clearance meant she could move freely after hours. Around-the-clock TimeWire security watched the outer perimeter, but Lilet slept in the inner sanctum as she healed, within the octagon of rooms that housed MADRINA and other ongoing TimeWire experiments. The TimePool slept in the center of the octagon, its waters turning and lapping at all times, so that as she neared the core (eight glass doors) she could see it, a black oval like a bathtub, four-foot tall walls, and above it the faint cast of waterlight, alternations in green. She could hear it too: a licking sound, cradling of a mother's womb. The doors parted for her and she stood alone beneath the dome.

Lilet breathed it in: the familiar encasement of metal and glass, cold air prickling her arms beneath the winglike material of the nightdress they'd given her. The room was always kept cold.

She didn't know if she could set the whole thing up herself. It would probably take most of the night. She would certainly get caught. She might get stuck in Avila's consciousness, might find halfway through that it was actually impossible to consciousness-travel entirely on her own.

But Lilet would try. She was already wearing her TimeSuit underneath the nightdress. She slipped it off and it fluttered to the ground, and she moved toward the light feeling mothlike and new, like she'd found something she never expected to find. She'd been told she might find it, but hadn't known she would want the connection so badly: her own madrina. A woman of her bloodline.

*

*Tell me about this controversy. So many people went through the project—it was hard to retain people. I imagine there are different facets to that.*

Yes, there are, but maybe not as many as you'd think. The screening process was intensive because you needed someone in an extremely stable mental state. The mental risks involved in consciousness travel were innumerable ... disassociation, erroneous memory, depression, paranoia, PTSD in participants who traveled into women who lived in violent times and circumstances. We witnessed extreme, debilitating forms of homesickness, people who developed a crippling need for a place they'd never actually known.

You're also putting the body through a kind of trauma: keeping it at low temperature, penetrating the skin, keeping the body wet. If you ate in someone else's body, you sometimes felt, upon return, as if you'd eaten. And your mind would tell your body that it didn't want to eat again. Participants developed highly irregular patterns. For awhile the

175

average was three trips, before we retired someone from the program. We retired at the earliest warning signs; we ran a full assessment on each participant after every trip. Not everyone wanted to quit and in some cases, that was another problem: addiction.

When I started traveling, I found that I was good at it. I could keep my body, my mind over *here*, and their body, their mind over *there*. My final assessments were free and clear. My team was astounded from the beginning, and then my ability became immensely valuable to them. Because I could start to recognize through-lines. I could compare trips to previous trips, from my own perspective. I could speak to trends and changes. And I liked learning. People are messy, complicated, emotional, but as an anthropologist I could approach that messiness in a methodological way.

Anyway. About the termination process.

*My understanding is that immediate termination from the project happened if … the participant ended up in the mind of someone they knew?*

Not someone they knew. I don't actually think anyone ended up *that* close in time, that they knew the person. No. What we encountered was that, because consciousness travel paired you with people who already shared strong mental affinity, you would, at some point, inevitably, end up in your own bloodline. In the consciousness of your own ancestor. People who encountered this knew it immediately, irrevocably, pit-of-the-stomach. They came out of that pool changed when it happened. We called it finding your own madrina. Keep in mind that the acronym means godmother.

*Wow. That seems like a dwooning experience.*

I don't...

*Here on Katla, if the moon and sun are up at the same time, you get a bizarre light around them. It's purple. It kind of sparkles. And it's really unsettling for some people. They have an actual reaction to it. So something that gives you that unsettled feeling, all the way down to your bones, it's dawn-mooning, dwooning.*

To my ear it's a slightly silly word.

*We use a lot of words that I think will sound silly to you here.*

Fair. So ... once ... dwooned ... participants would snap. They had an insatiable need to go back. They'd try to break into TimeWire. They wanted their madrina's conversation, her guidance, they wanted to know their family secrets and truths. At that point, we couldn't risk it. People were not stable enough to travel again. Either they weren't stable enough or—like we found the one time we allowed a participant to go on one trip after the fact—the emotional tether was too strong. She'd pop right back in to that same person, that same body, the same location even. Her mind became too targeted.

*Wouldn't that be useful? You said earlier that you never had enough time to really get a sense for context.*

To be honest, no. It got too personal.

*But you were the most stable of them all.*

And so I tried to keep it a secret that I'd found her. Because I needed to see her again, and I knew I could handle a trip back. Or I thought I could.

## Part VI: Light
### 27 October 3011

"Welcome back. You missed the lanterns."

Avila carried an armful of damp, fern-like leaves that plastered against their joint forearms. The two of them, Avila and Lilet-in-Avila, walked in a loose pack of people. It seemed Lilet would always meet Avila at crepuscular times: she had arrived first at dusk, and now at dawn.

The forest path was mulch beneath them. Avila's sky-dclan—her people, her children, Lilet still didn't know exactly—circulated around them, playing, talking. The stone house that Lilet had seen before in Avila's memory stood ahead of them on the path now, embraced by trees that looked deciduous, that had a bluish tint to their leaves. Those leaves, the size of a large, splayed hand, hung low over the house and obscured its borders, framed its wooden front door.

"Shhhh," said Avila.

Lilet nodded lightly. She and Avila both know that they couldn't speak with the same mouth in public. Lilet always remained cognizant of the rules of consciousness travel: stay as inauspicious as possible. Do not endanger the madrina, do not make her appear insane, do not make her behave in a highly unconventional way for their circumstances. So Lilet took the opportunity to have Avila look around and study the people around her.

They all wore floor-length, skirted garments woven in jeweled earth tones. In place of shoes they wore the luminescent bioskins designed in the 2200s. Their feet shone in the dawn, but not a harsh light. They could see where they were going and their feet were encased in the most natural, hearty protection, not getting pricked by spines that came up through the forest floor. Most adults carried foliage, space baskets that compressed their bounty as well as regular woven baskets full of bulb vegetables.

Even though they weren't speaking, Lilet could sense Avila trying to soothe her confusion. Where on Earth were they?

A word cropped up in their consciousness: *heimagar*. Lilet felt the impressions of that word. Homeland, homeplace, heartplace.

Homeland, homeplace, heartplace. Lilet exchanged a word from her childhood: *hogar*.

"Old word," said Avila out loud.

Lilet could have asked the natural follow-up question (*how old*). She could have done many things in that forest, with those people, but she wouldn't that day.

She was yanked away from Avila just as they were about to enter the house.

Would there never be enough time, never, would there always be another house she barely missed? Before the world became a dark tunnel, Lilet noticed something familiar mounted to the left of the door: an intermittent red light. It looked like Bailey tech, like an alarm light from the ship. As Avila reached her hand out the door tech blinked green, just like it would on the Bailey. The kind of tech that knew you, that managed to feel personal.

*

They hadn't even bothered to turn all the lights on when they pulled her out. To their credit, they were gentle, even if scared and angry.

Lilet emerged to find her team circulating around her in a dark flurry. Low glow of bioskins, glint of glass, shadow of their bodies all in motion, the misplaced *beep beeeeeeep* of the temperature gauge, water on the floor. Nadya's voice carried orders and the team fed her data: *We have three rent TimeWires. Bath volume low! She's breathing!*

Lilet *was* breathing. On the medical cot she'd been transferred to, lying on her back. Dabo's Ayelid was blinking green just above his eyes.

"I should have told you," she said.

He didn't look her in the eye.

But she motioned him close, and he bent down reluctantly. They gazed at each other, and his hand instinctively moved a slimy strand of her hair from her eyes.

"You can't tell anyone," she whispered. "What I have to tell you."

"What is it?"

But she swooned then, and his face blackened and closed. She didn't have a clear grasp on what she wanted to say anyway.

## Part VII: Location
### *27 October 3011*

After being pulled from the TimePool, Lilet no longer stayed in the luxury of the station bed. She was moved to a holding cell in BailJail (technically the Josiph Möller Detention Center), a place where the metal of the floor breathed cold up through her socks. It was a perfectly clean cube, her cell. Blue-tinged. Crisp corners. Stainless. The bed was a thick plate that *zooooohhhmed* out from the wall come nighttime. The back wall of the cube was a light-wall that emanated softly, a small comfort.

She got bored and anxious within an hour of being led to holding. Nadya had brought her here, saying nothing on that interminable walk, her arm looped through Lilet's as if they were intimate friends rather than captive and captor. Nadya said nothing until they were close and then she turned on Lilet, dwarfing her.

"Jesus Fucksaturn, Lilet," she said. "The Bailey is *lost* and we *needed* you."

"I know we're lost," said Lilet.

*

MADRINA had resulted in a few positive location stamps. One of those had been Lilet's. She'd stamped them back to Lima, Perú, when she'd entered a woman who lived there in the 1940s, chosen off the street for her gleaming black hair to be the face of a shampoo ad. Lilet had entered her consciousness the moment she stood in front of her own ad, peeling off the back of a window at the neighborhood hair salon. The madrina had never seen herself photographed before. She stood there, looking at her own bare shoulders, the sleeves that barely cropped up, and suddenly she was arrested by dread, wondering what the men in her family would say, hoping that they wouldn't see it even though they walked by the salon every day.

Lilet remembered how enthusiastically they'd entered the Peruvian coordinates at CC. She also remembered the balloon deflation of the room when the coordinates blinked on a hovering black holo, the word *unknown* radiating around them. Only darkness. As she looked out at the gleaming black of space, Lilet remembered the madrina's hair.

*

Dabo came by, three hours in. He found her sitting cross-legged perpendicular to the light-bars, braiding the sparse black of her own hair.

"Maybe I was entranced," she said, without really looking up.

"Lilet," he lamented. "By what."

She looked up, smiled at his gentleness, wondering if her love for him was just her looking for a soft wing in a floating steel world. Grounding where there was no ground.

"The location stamps have all failed," she said. "We haven't been able to route back to Earth. We're too far. Butterfly. *Butterfly.* We can't flap our wings back home."

"You shouldn't be in here," he said. "Who do I talk to? Nadya?"

"It messes with my brain when they yank me out like that."

His hand hovered near the bars. She knew how desperately he wanted to reach through.

*

"We have to shut down MADRINA, Lilet. CC gave us a timeframe to find Earth and we're past it."

They sat in a white-walled room on either end of a long table. Behind Nadya's head, a depth-holo screen glistened. Lilet's Ayelid synced with it.

"There was more of a purpose to MADRINA, Nadya," Lilet said. She blinked, and the screen behind Nadya displayed it: a stillphoto of their original collective, smiling, ringing the TimePool. Nadya pursed her lips and Lilet

182

blinked again, changing the image to a slideshow of the madrinas; they'd been able to find photo and video of some of the people they'd traveled into.

"It's become all about finding Earth," Lilet continued. "But that's not what it used to be. We didn't develop location stamping til midway through and now we're trying to invent as we go along."

"We did have a purpose," said Nadya, turning away from the screen. "Had. But hey you know what? I bet, at some point, we would've ended up in a woman right at the border. Someone living in one of those final foreclosed cities of earth. Then we would've known our hell-history. We would've known exactly how much we wasted and destroyed and burnt up."

"So the narratives and emotional reality of human history are useless to us?"

"Yes, because we are *buying time* to exist. Are you used to it yet? The idea of dying in space?"

"Maybe Earth is too far at this point," said Lilet. "Did you think of that? The accidental jump could've taken us years past Katla."

"Of course. But what else are we going to stamp to if we're using consciousness travel instead of communication? When do we stop? When you're dead? And all the new women we vet? Dead women talking to dead women because they wanted to fill in a broken map."

"You relied on me too much."

"And you were worth it until a nice lake got involved."

"Just because I recovered every time you broke me open doesn't mean I didn't break."

A radiating quiet. There were no windows in the room.

"I'm sorry," said Nadya.

"I'm so tired of looking out the windows and seeing this sheet of nothing and nowhere," said Lilet, allowing the wall to revert to black.

"I've been tired since I was born."

"I remember," said Lilet. "When I'd see a planet far away and get excited. Look how corporeal it is. How *real*. But it was never Katla."

"We're baboons out here. We're snails. How is it possible no one on the whole ship can figure out where we are. *How*."

"Did anyone even try to get a location stamp on me?"

"The first time obviously. Nothing came up. Full Earth scan and nothing even lit up as likely. And we focused Nordic. The second time we were too busy saving all of our tech because it wasn't meant to be manned by one person."

"You say you're shutting it all down anyway, so who cares. Give me one more chance."

"You'll go into the same person and you'll stop breathing again."

"So let me stop breathing."

"Deathshitwish, Lilet."

"I've been thinking about it and I think that if you keep me in there long enough, I'm confident that you'll get a location stamp."

"Your madrina doesn't make Earth any closer or location stamping any more sophisticated."

"You're not going to stamp me to Earth. You're going to stamp me to Katla."

Nadya blinked, and her voice became smaller.

"Descendant?"

## Part VIII: Descendant
*10 November 3011*

They were being lowered together into familiar water.

The hands that held them—utmost gentleness, careful fingers—were familiar too, at least to Avila. And the place was familiar. The light. The trees had somewhat shifted color, become bluer, though the water, when they tilted their mutual head to the right, was green as ever.

"May you always have beginning and end. May your feet always touch the ground. May you always find haven."

These were the words that Avila spoke to the circle of faces above her, some tearful, others ashen. Too many faces for Lilet to internalize. One person had green-hued skin and white hair, and dabbed at dark eyes.

Avila's vocal chords were dry and withered. Lilet could feel the immediate difference, the withering of their entire body. She had never entered the consciousness of someone so much older than her. She wondered if this was how it felt for some to become old, a vital mind trapped inside of a body that felt like a shell.

"Strange way to put it," muttered Avila. The ring of mourners had turned their backs to her ceremoniously and were walking away, disturbing the water.

"What did you come here for?" asked Lilet. Though she knew. Her weak heart seized.

"This is my deathday," said Avila. "We know ahead of time. Don't be concerned."

"I've never been inside of a dying body," said Lilet.

"I'm sorry. You won't be with me when I die. We know ahead of time. Also, you wouldn't be so rude as to stay here with me when I die. You saw how everyone else left. Death is a private matter. Who wants to see or hear anyone but their deepest self at the end?"

Avila had come back to the waterfall to feel like her deepest self. Here, her thin arms floated. Pain that radiated in her hips and shoulders soothed, at least a little. Her skydclan had known to bring her here.

"Something strange happens in your mind when I think the word *family*," said Lilet.

"That's because we don't understand family the same way, Lilet. You're still labeling blood relation. But the people I think of as relatives, my skydclan, are all chosen."

"None of those children were yours?"

"I didn't give birth to them. I found them, like I find wildberries by morning."

"So you mean…"

"Yes, Lilet. I am sorry. I'm the one dying, you will continue living, and yet I'm here to comfort you."

"I'm going to have children."

"And they're going to have children and children. This is the end of only one of your lines; who knows how far your other branches reach?"

"You aren't my madrina. You're my ahijada."

"You're weakening our voice. But you can think to me. You just have to learn to listen to my thoughts in return. They might be colors and feelings, but you speak that language. Yes. We learn the color code. Oatgrass. Twilight."

Lilet felt so tired in Avila's body. She couldn't fathom leaving, standing again, doing anything but resting. *What do I do now?*

Avila's thoughts came back like a starburst.

*They found it already, while you were here talking to me.*

*I want to keep talking to you.*

*You thought that MADRINA would be about finding your lost godmothers in the past,* said Avila. *They were like fairies to you. But now you know: you too are godmother. Not only finding the world that was, but creating the world that will be.*

*I want this to be my reality now.*

*I know. But now you have to let me sleep, butterfly.*

*

When she came back to her body, the first things she recognized were her pounding head and bloodless arms, which had gone numb and crossed over her chest in an X in the time she hadn't been breathing properly. The room around her vibrated with confused energy.

The plane in front of her eyes blinked with tech-light, in and out of darkness as her body was eased from the pool. A hushed path opened for her, and the world changed orientation as Nadya and Dabo carried her to the waiting cot.

The room was full of people she probably knew. Somewhere, a whisper rose to a wordless howl of joy, and then laughter and sound and applause erupted around her and made her head and eyes pound. She shook her head, mouthing *stop*. She closed her eyes, opened them, and saw Dabo as he inclined her bed to sitting. She noticed that Dabo had tears in his eyes.

Lilet thought she might faint. She felt like her body floated somewhere else and wasn't actually her body. She wanted water but couldn't summon the language to ask for it. Before she knew it, she had reverted to her first words, mouthing *agua*.

Nadya disappeared, a shadow gone from her side, and returned with a cup that she lifted to Lilet's lips. Lilet drank, though the first few sips hurt her throat.

The room had gone quiet and parted for her again, a red sea. When she looked up through the pathway that opened, she saw a beautiful, solid holo. It looked like a miniature planet, opaque and detailed enough to touch, floating in the air between them. A silver tinge to its atmosphere: its water appeared grey, but a stately slate-grey, not grim or murky. A blue tinge to its earth.

"We aren't far, Lilet," said Dabo. "This whole time, we weren't far."

Once again, she couldn't find the language. She couldn't even say the word. She started to heave and cry, unsure if tears were coming from her eyes or not, and the whole room cried with her and laughed and clapped. Their bodies sang with sound.

*Katla.*

Part IX: Waterfall
*4 June 3015*

*The M.A.D.R.I.N.A Project Casebooks: Mimicry Anthropology through Direct Reallocation and Intertemporal-Substitution by Neural Affinity*

Verbal Agreement 00:00 - 00:10 - 4 June 3015
Entry by Lilet DeEsparza, Ph.D

*My name is Dr. Lilet DeEsparza. I am a participant in the MADRINA Project. This is our first casebook entry to setup transition of MADRINA from the Bailey to Katla. First priority will be syncing assimilated data with our contact team EM-1 back on Earth, now that we have established communication again. EM-1 was keen to archive sociological data generated by MADRINA.*

*Our current timeline involves keeping MADRINA tech on board the landed Bailey for the remainder of scheduled trials, then to move to a secure location after we source one. Our new Katla-based team is enthusiastic to help us find such a space, though, understandably, very little has been constructed on Katla yet. We may also work remotely with Earth architects and Katla-based design teams to invest in designing a custom TimePool lab for MADRINA.*

*We are ready for our work to continue.*

Verbal Agreement 00:00 - 00:13 - 4 June 3015
Entrev. Coady Ka-Vera, Katla MCOMM, c/ Lilet DeEsparza, Ph.D

*I'm a child of Katla. Second generation post-Noptera. The arrival of the Bailey was something we anticipated for years. The first settlement team here was only that: settlement. A sampling of Katlan specialists and citizens with Oran certification. All our tech essentially came from the dismantled ship. My parents built from scraps and learned to live off the land again. We were paving the way for you, the real heroes of the story.*

What's it like for you, learning about Earth? A world you never knew?

*Earth is a fantasy to me. A dark and glorious and decayed and beautiful dream.*

A containment field of history. It felt that way to me too. Only, Katla also felt that way. It's like I was born in a gap. Like my whole life is a transition between people who will have true lives.

*But aren't you happy to have landed?*

Of course. I've seen the promised land. Who wouldn't be happy? But it doesn't feel *mine.*

*You haven't been here very long.*

I've been going back to the Bailey just to feel like myself.

*Isn't there any part of Katla that you've started to feel an attachment to? Or even an attraction to? I know you toured our settlement.*

There is one place. I just haven't been there yet.

*

It took pulling up the initial location stamp.

A strange afternoon: Lilet, Dabo, and Nadya onboard the Bailey again a month post-landing. The TimePool room that had taken on a sleepy, rusted feeling, even though it was still used every few days. Lilet herself hadn't used it. She hadn't used TimeWire since her last visit with Avila.

Dabo was rubbing his hands and scratching at his scalp. He'd dealt with a slew of allergic reactions since arriving on Katla. Lilet suspected it was from the fibers of Katlan clothes, which he still insisted on wearing. They'd all had their new things since coming to Katla, things that made

190

them new people. Dabo, always the pleaser, had a need to be Katlan, and he marked this by the clothes he wore. So Nadya and Lilet stood in black and red Bailey suits while Dabo wore draped beige layers.

"You look like a monk," said Lilet.

Dabo's dimples started to show: his distinct grin that preceded a joke. "In the gardens of the Noptera settlement there's a crinkly little turnip," he said. "There's a grub that guards the turnip bulb, and it glows and blinks red. Biolu-minescent! The entomologists can't wait to figure it all out."

Nadya had turned on the tech and the room hummed dreamily to life. A red light pulsed somewhere. "Is that what I look like?" asked Lilet.

"That's what you look like," said Dabo.

She beamed for him, trying hard to erase insincerity from her face. He looked away from her to swear and scratch his hands. For the first time, Lilet felt a pulsing sad-ness, a part of her life blinking away. It was the first time she didn't get the joke.

"Got it," barked Nadya, her voice stressed and utilitari-an as ever. Since their arrival, Nadya had taken the helm on assimilated and assigning scientists to different habitation zones in the Noptera settlement.

And Lilet? She hadn't settled anywhere yet. The endless desire for interviews and conversations (as the face of the Bailey's "Katlan Salvation") overwhelmed her, left her feel-ing like a drifting, stripped leaf. So she drifted back and forth between the settlement that felt like a fantasy zone and the empty, cavernous Bailey. She walked its halls and recognized herself in the echo of her own footsteps. She felt her way through the darkness and imagine being swallowed by a whale.

"Lilet. Did you hear me? I found your waterfall."

*

They offered to go with her but she wanted to go alone.

The hike took two hours. Two Bailey hours, equivalent to four Earth hours. Lilet wasn't accustomed to Katlan hours yet.

Two Bailey hours of battling steep, muddy, unmarked ground that rose through a forest on an incline east of Noptera. Dabo had given her a location injection so that he and Nadya could keep track of her from the Bailey. At the beginning of the hike, trees with blue trunks and fanning turquoise leaves scattered the cold light of the Katlan sun. Red and blue worms gnawed at leaf-mulch beneath her feet (and hands, when she had to crawl). The tree limbs warped and dipped in knots; she hadn't noticed them much in Avila's body, maybe because Avila didn't notice them.

Lilet turned her Ayelid off. Avila hadn't (wouldn't) use one, and Lilet wanted to experience all of this with unencumbered eyes.

The air felt dewy. After an hour of climbing, the incline leveled out and the ecosystem shifted. Trees emerged barkless; their trunks and branches shiny-smooth, charcoal-black. Lilet stood breathless at the sight of them, tunneling away from her. Their leaves were emerald snowflakes. Diamonds of light fell on the fern-lapped ground. Sun rays twinkled white.

Beyond the trees, she saw a wall of stone and shadow shrouded by white mist: the first hint of cliff and water.

*

There was always a discrepancy between the sensory experience of being inside a madrina and being in her own body. Even if sensations felt vivid while in the madrina, they were always more vivid when experienced firsthand.

And so the waterfall assaulted her with its color, its fullness, its size.

The slate cliffs surrounded the pool in a towering promenade carpeted by Katlan ferns and mosses, interspersed with low canopy trees. The white spray of the falls broke through at different intervals along the cliffs and cascaded to meet the waters she knew so well. Someday Avila would be born near these waters. She would float on her back and look up at the sun in her billowing white shirt and speak to Lilet for the first time. Later, she would choose this place for her most private, internal moment, her deathday, and Lilet would be the last person she spoke to.

Lilet walked forward. Wet leaves draped and tickled her shins. This was Katlan springtime, and she wore thin black stretch pants from the Bailey through which she could feel the leaves. They grew dense as she approached the water's edge. When the water kissed her fingers, thick and silt-laden as she remembered, she felt an ache she hadn't felt before, something she didn't even feel when returning to the sanctuary of the Bailey. The ache of return. Homeland, homeplace, heartplace.

Lilet stood, turned, and looked back the way she came. She could picture it now: the clearing, the stone walls, the Bailey tech blinking at the door, the arms that encircled other arms and carried goods in preparation for a meal.

As she imagined the future, Lilet no longer felt she was drifting. She had found the home-that-would-be, and there was much to build.

"Madrina" will appear in *The Latinx Archive: Speculative Fiction for Dreamers,* publication anticipated in 2019.

# In a Manner of Speaking
by Charity Tahmaseb

I use the last of the good candles to build the radio. I still have light. The fire burns, and there is a never-ending supply of the cheap, waxy candles in the storeroom. I will—eventually—burn through all of those. My fire will die. The cold will invade this space.

But today I have a radio. Today I will speak to the world—or what's left of it. I compare my radio to the picture in the instructions. It looks the same, but not all the steps had illustrations. This troubles me. My radio may not work.

I crank the handle to charge the battery. This feels good. This warms my arms, and I must take deep breaths to keep going. I shake out my hand and crank some more. When buzz and static fill my ears, I nearly jump. That, too, sounds warm. I am so used to the cold. The creak and groan of ice, the howl of the wind. These cold sounds are their own kind of silence. They hold nothing warm or wet or alive.

I decide on a frequency for no other reason than I like the number. I press the button on the mouthpiece. This, according to the instructions, will let the world hear me.

"Hello?" My voice warbles and I leap back, as if something might spring from the speakers.

Nothing does, of course. In fact, nothing happens at all. It takes more than one try to reach the world.

"Hello? Hello? Is anyone there? Can you hear me? I would like to talk to you."

Perhaps I should try another frequency—or try a little patience. If someone is out there with a radio, might they right now be cranking a handle to charge a battery, or sleeping, or adding wood to their fire? This last is something I must do and soon. The embers grow a bright orange, but the chill has invaded the edges of the room.

That means venturing outside. Of all the chores, I like this one the least. The trek to the shed is short, but nothing lights my way. The dark is just that: dark. While the cold is fierce, I know nothing can lurk outside my shelter, waiting to pounce. And yet, every time I collect wood, it's as if a predator stalks me. I anticipate claws digging into my shoulder, sharp teeth at my neck, my spine cracked in half.

But the only thing outside my shelter is the cold. But it is the cold that will take me in the end. So in a sense, I am its prey and it is stalking me.

With my parka buttoned tight, I clip myself to the rope between my shelter and the shed. Wind tears at me, and I plod to the shed. I pat the pile of wood, reassured that yes, it is substantial. For now. With my arms full, I push against the wind and spill into the shelter.

It's then I hear something. At first, I don't recognize it because it's been so long since I've heard that sound. Then the notion of it lights my mind. I fly across the room, wood spilling from my arms, the wind banging the door behind me.

It's a voice.

I grab the mouthpiece, my thumb clumsy through wool mittens.

"Hello! Hello! Are you there? Can you hear me? Hello?"

The wind screams at my back. The door slams against the wall, the noise like a death knell.

"Please. Talk to me."

My small space is chaos. Whirling snow, slamming door, biting wind, and scattered wood. It is too loud and too cold for anyone to hear me over the radio, and I have foolishly let the heat escape. It will take hours to warm the air to the point where I can sit without my body convulsing with shivers.

I have been so very foolish.

I fight the wind to shut the door. With it latched, I turn to inspect the mess. Stoke the fire first. Perhaps by the time I stack the wood and sweep the debris, the flames will throw enough heat that I can sit, crank the radio, and try again.

After I clean, after I heat my insides with broth, I crank the handle and try the radio again. I send my voice into the endless night, into the world, maybe even the universe. My voice could go on forever, long after I am gone. But that doesn't seem to matter.

No one answers.

*

When I wake, my nose is chilled, but only slightly. The air holds enough warmth that I can move and think. The fire is hungry, I can tell, but content to give me heat for the moment. Last night's folly has not ruined anything. My gaze lands on the radio, and I wonder. Is it more of a curse than a possible blessing?

I will try again today. It will not hurt to try. It will keep me warm and keep me busy. As long as I don't hope too much, it cannot hurt me, either.

After I eat a can of peaches for breakfast, I set to the task of cranking the handle and giving the battery a full charge. I debate switching frequencies. I wonder if that voice I heard was merely wishful thinking. These thoughts do not stop my thumb from pressing the button.

"Hello? Are you there? I think I heard you last night. Well, it's always night here. I mean, before. I heard you before."

Even now, without the sun, I still think in night and day, breakfast and dinner. I could have broth for breakfast, but I never do. I could reconstitute eggs and eat them for dinner, but again, I never do. I am a creature of habits. Now, these habits are all I have left.

"Is there anyone there?" I speak slowly, in case these words must fight the static to reach whoever is on the other side. "Should I change frequencies?"

This seems to be a silly question. If no one has answered my other calls, I'm not certain why this would compel them to. My fingers touch the dial. I'm about to spin it when something crackles over the speaker.

"No."

I stare at the space in front of the radio as if it's possible to see the owner of this voice.

"No?" My reply is a tiny thing.

"Don't ... don't change the frequency ... there's a good girl. Hold tight, I'm having some technical difficulties, but I'm here."

"I don't understand. You can hear me?"

"I can hear you."

"You have a radio too?"

"In a manner of speaking. I have a way to talk to your radio, at least."

Again, I stare at the space in front of the radio. I even wave a hand in the air. The voice is so rich and deep and clear. Yes, there is no static on my frequency. I wonder if that is something this other voice has done.

"Are you a man?" I ask.

"In a manner of speaking."

I laugh. The button on the mouthpiece is still depressed, so this voice, this man, hears my laughter. His own in response is as rich as his voice.

"I don't know what that means," I say.

"I don't either, except that I was a man, once—or male, at least. If that makes sense," he says, his reply filled with both humor and sadness. "Now I am, perhaps, less than that."

I still don't understand, but I'm not certain it matters. Not when there's a voice on the other side of this endless night, not when that voice wants to talk to me.

"I'm Soshi," I say, a strange, unaccountable shyness invading my voice and heating my cheeks.

"It's a pleasure to meet you, Soshi. I am Jatar."

I like the way his name feels in my mouth, and I say it out loud. "Jatar." Yes, it is delicious. Speaking is delicious. I touch my cheeks. The skin burns hot, but my fingers are like ice. The fire. Too late, I realize I've let it die down far too much.

"Oh, no," I murmur. "I forgot about the fire."

"Go, go. Tend to your fire. Then fix yourself something to eat, and come back and charge your battery. I will be here, on this frequency."

"Always? When I call, you will be there?"

"In these times, Soshi, there aren't many things I can promise. But I will promise you this. I will always be on this frequency, and I will always hear your call."

*

Jatar won't talk to me until I've assured him that I've fed myself, tended to the fire, and the other chores. How he knows I need to do these things puzzles me. Of course, I did fling my words into the darkness before we found each other. So I ask him.

"Yes," he says. "I did hear you. I have trouble on my end. Your radio is nothing like the device I use."

"You still have trouble?"

"Had. I mean, I had trouble. But you can hear me now, yes?"

"Yes." Sometimes I want to nod or smile, but I know he can't see these things. We have nothing but voices to guide us—their tone, their thickness or thinness. How a smile makes the throat warm and disapproval has an edge.

"You are not on earth," I say, "are you?"

The frequency carries his sigh to me, and the sound holds reluctance. "No, I am not."

"You are lucky then."

"I don't know about that."

"Where are you?"

"I don't know about that, either." By the way he says this, I know he wants me to laugh.

I do, but I also want to know the answer. "Where are you?"

"I'm not certain *where* matters all that much, not anymore."

"But you must be somewhere."

"Must I, dear girl? Must I really?"

I don't know how to answer that. I crank the handle to charge the battery, just so I don't lose the connection. I hate that, every morning—or what I call morning—charging the battery, sprouting sweat, and praying that Jatar's voice will come over the speaker and fill my little room with warmth.

"Maybe you are in my radio," I say now.

This time, he laughs. "What I wouldn't give to be there, living inside your radio."

"You would have to be very small," I say. "Smaller than a mouse."

"You wouldn't need to feed me very much."

No, I wouldn't. A thought seizes me. I think of small things, tiny things, mouse-sized things. I think of their absence.

"I killed them," I say. The confession both lifts me up and weighs on me. I know its truth.

Our frequency is clear of buzz and static. So when there's silence, it stretches long and empty.

"Who do you think you've killed," Jatar says at last, his words quiet and low.

"The mice. When I first … found this place, there were droppings everywhere. The food is in metal containers and on metal shelves. But I stopped leaving crumbs. No more crumbs, no more mice."

"And it's you, not the lack of sun or heat that's responsible."

"I don't need to eat every last crumb."

A few nights ago, I left a bit of cracker on the floor, deliberately. I placed it well away from my sleeping pallet. My first nights in this space, I was consumed with the fear of mice, of rats, crawling over me in my sleep. I jerked awake so many times, breathing hard, cold sweat washing across my skin that I almost gave up on sleeping. But this time, when I woke, the crumb remained, untouched.

"Oh, dear girl, you did not kill the mice. They no doubt went elsewhere. They are resourceful creatures. Besides, they carry diseases. They could contaminate your food, your water…"

Jatar's voice fades, either from the buzzing in my head or failing battery power. I remember standing over that crumb, then falling on my knees next to it. For how long I stared, I don't know. Here's what I do know:

I picked it up and ate it.

"I can't talk now, Jatar," I say into the mouthpiece.

"Soshi, please. Listen to me, you did not kill the mice." Jatar's voice fills the air. He does not stop talking, not even when I refuse to respond. "You'll lose me soon if you don't crank the handle." He knows the life of the battery—or at least how to gauge it. "Crank the handle, at least. Tell me you're still with me."

But I don't. I sit, curled by the fire, chin on my knees. I could've captured a mouse, tempted it with some crumbs, built a home for it, close enough to the fire so it would always be warm. We would dine together, morning and night. I could spare what it would need to survive. I would have given it a good mouse name.

But I don't have a mouse. Something about that makes me clutch my legs to my chest. Salt from tears irritates my cheeks, but it's only later, when the tracks have dried, that I scrub my face with my palms. I've forgotten to eat, and the fire is low, but it's the radio that I reach for. My chest heaves as I crank the handle.

"Jatar," I say when there's enough power to carry my voice. "I want a mouse."

"I know you do, dear girl. I know you do."

He is there; he is always there. Maybe he does live in my radio. Maybe Jatar is my mouse.

"I know you do," he says one last time. His sigh carries so much weight I'm surprised the air isn't thick with the sound. "Your fire," he prompts.

"I should stoke it."

"Dinner?"

"Not yet."

"Tend to your chores. I'll be here when you're done."

"You will?"

"Where else would I go?"

*

I have found a rubber band, one that feels stretchy and fresh in my fingers. Its edges have not rotted away. It is strong, and when I wrap it around the mouthpiece, the button remains depressed. I love my radio, but now I am no longer tethered to it. I can use both hands while talking to Jatar.

Not that he can see my hands. But I can stoke the fire, feed myself, and crank the handle. I can fall silent, and he will not worry—too much. He can hear the rustle of my boots against the floor, the whisper of the broom, the crack and sizzle when I stoke the fire.

"Have you gathered wood recently?" he asks now.

"Last night … yesterday. It's stacked high. I don't dare bring anymore in for a while."

The air is too dry; sparks from the fire have too great a range. The thing that keeps me alive can also kill me. At least then I'd be warm, I tell myself. I don't speak these words to Jatar, but my laugh gives me away.

"That sounds morbid."

"It is," I admit. "I was thinking about the fire, how it might kill me before the cold does."

"I wish you wouldn't—"

"It's like that poem about the world ending in fire and ice. And I think it could be both, couldn't it?"

"I suppose it could, and suppose we change the subject?"

I agree, but don't know what to say at first. Jatar does not talk much about himself, although I wish he would. That doesn't stop me from trying.

"Can you see the stars where you are?" I ask.

"On occasion, yes, I can."

"Ours left. Actually, that's not right. I'm guessing they're still in the sky."

"Your guess would be correct."

"We blotted them out, all the stars, our sun, and now we have nothing. You know, when I first found this place, you could still see the stars from here. I thought: *oh, I am so lucky*. There used to be a stream. It even had fish, although they swam funny, so I never ate them."

"That seems like a wise decision."

His words have a teasing quality that makes me want to talk more so I can hear the humor and approval in his tone.

"It must have been a beautiful spot, with the mountains and the woods. I wonder why no one else ever came up after I did. Was it just too late?"

"Perhaps they weren't as smart as you."

"I don't think that's it. I think something happened, but I just don't know what that something is."

"Hm." Jatar sounds as if he's giving this much thought. "It's possible that the only thing to happen was self-inflicted, especially with the cities, as crowded as they were. Disease, fighting. It's hard to say."

"The cities *were* crowded. It's why we left." I nod before stopping myself, since Jatar can't see me. I may be the only witness to these things, and yet, I might as well be blind for all I've seen. Self-inflicted. The phrase makes me think of something else I found along the stream, something else I witnessed, and yet didn't.

"I'm wearing a dead woman's boots," I say.

I must shock Jatar with this confession. Silence greets me, and I wonder if I need to crank the handle again. At long last, he coughs.

"Dear girl, Soshi … I don't know what you mean by that."

"When there was still some sunlight, when I could walk along the stream, I found a body, a skeleton, really. Small, like me, so I'm guessing it was a woman. She was mostly bones, but the gun was still in her hand, and for some reason, nothing had chewed away the boots on her feet. Thick leather. They're heavy, but they are very good boots."

"The boots on her feet." Jatar says these words slowly. "Your boots?"

"I had to shake her bones from them, but yes. I took her boots."

"Did you leave her gun?"

"By that time, there was nothing left to shoot. I didn't see the point, even though I was still scared. I didn't think anyone would climb up this high in the mountains, not if they hadn't already."

"So you left the gun." Jatar's voice is tight as if this is something he absolutely must know.

"I left the gun," I say. "What would I shoot at? The wind? What would that do? Maybe cause an avalanche?"

"Yes, I suppose it could." He clears his throat. "I don't like this subject either."

"Then you tell me something about you."

"I am not that interesting."

"Are you a scientist?"

Jatar is intelligent; I can tell he holds back in saying things, perhaps so I don't feel bad for not being all that smart myself.

"A scientist?" he says. "Is that what you think I am?"

"You are very smart."

"I don't know about that, but you could call me a scientist, in a manner of speaking."

I sigh. The radio carries the sound to wherever Jatar is, and he laughs.

"What do you study? Planets? Stars? Solar systems?"

"Yes, you could say that. I ... take the temperature of things. Some of those things include stars and planets."

"Earth?"

There's the slightest hitch in our frequency, the slightest bit of hesitation in his voice. "No, actually, Earth wasn't something I monitored."

"But you are now?"

"On my own time."

"You must have a lot of time."

Here, he laughs, the sound so clear and hearty, I can't help but laugh as well.

"Oh, yes, I do," he says. "I have time to spare."

*

"I wish I knew what day it was," I say.

I am trying to draw Jatar out, get him to respond. Today he has been so very quiet.

"I always know what day it is," he says.

"Somehow, I don't think it's the same as mine."

"It is, and it isn't."

"Because if I knew what day it was, we could have a party."

"What kind of party?"

"Well, that depends on the day. See? It's important."

His laugh filters through the speakers.

"It could even be my birthday."

"Oh, dear girl, it certainly could. You deserve lots of birthday parties."

"Would you get me a present?"

"As many as I could carry to you."

"Like what?"

"How about a mouse?"

"I would very much like a mouse. I would name it Jatar."

A harrumph comes from the speakers, one so strong the radio seems to vibrate with it.

"I think," Jatar says, his words slow, "that I should be offended."

Before I can explain that having a mouse named after you is an honor, the floorboards shake beneath my feet. I give a little cry, no more than a yelp from the back of my throat, but Jatar hears.

"What is it?" he demands.

"I don't know. The house is…"

I can't find words to describe the tremors that run through it. It's like my house has suddenly caught a fever and is shaking with chills. Then there's an awful groan.

"Oh, dear girl," Jatar says, and now his voice is low, but taut, as if it were nothing more than a rubber band stretched to its limits. "Stay by me—I mean, the radio. Stay by the radio. Do not open the door. Do not go outside. Stay as still and as quiet as you can."

I retreat to the radio, grip the mouthpiece, although I don't need to. Another groan sounds. It is like nothing I've heard, not even in the days when we fought to leave the city, and certainly my mountain has never made such noises.

"What is it?" I whisper, my lips only a breath away from the mouthpiece.

"I have heard this sound before."

"Will it eat me?"

"No." This word is not quite as tight as all his others. It almost sounds like he wants to laugh. "It won't eat you, dear girl."

The roar comes next, so loud it steals my breath. It reminds me of the few trains that still ran, back when we were walking, back before I was alone. We'd follow the tracks, and the roar would sneak up on you. Someone always kept watch.

Or did. Because, of course, the trains stopped running after a while. We still followed the tracks. They would lead us somewhere important, somewhere safe. I'm not sure how true that was, because they didn't lead me here, to my mountain, where I've been safe.

Until now.

The floorboards jump beneath my feet. The force knocks me into the wall and knocks embers from the fireplace. I claw my way across the floor. Before I can cup the glowing ember in my hands, I jerk back. I glance around, but the world shakes too hard, and my feet are too unsteady. Already smoke rises from the wood slats. I bite my lip and sacrifice the back of my left hand and shove the ember into the hearth.

I must scream. My throat aches as if I have. Jatar's voice pours from the speaker in response. He must fight to be heard over the roar and rumble and chaos that have swallowed my house.

Then, everything is quiet. The world. Jatar. So quiet I can hear the fire sputter. My gaze goes there first. Build the fire back up, make it safe. My left hand is nearly useless. If pain could scream, it would fill this space, this mountain, this world. I worry that I have done more damage than I can repair.

First things first. The fire. I build it up. I don't know if it's the stoked fire or if my hand makes me feel as if I'm on fire, but the air is warm, warmer than before. I glance about, knowing I must dig out some first aid supplies, perhaps scoop up some snow or ice from outside.

"Jatar?" I say, hoping to hear his voice.

Nothing.

Panic seizes me before I remember: the battery. It's an awkward thing, cranking the handle with my right hand, bracing the radio with my left elbow, but I manage it.

"Jatar?" I say, before I even have a full charge.

"Soshi? Dear girl, are you okay?"

"I burnt myself, but that's better than the house burning down. I'm going to get the first aid kit."

Actually, in the storeroom, I have many first aid kits, more than I could ever use.

"And maybe some snow," I add, making my way across the room. My legs wobble, and I take unsteady and erratic steps.

Behind me, Jatar is saying something, but he sounds so very far away. Shock, I think. How do I cure myself of that? Hand first, then the shock. I open the door to the outside. All I want to do is grope around, grab a handful of that sharp, crystalized mix of icy snow, and cool the fire of my skin.

At first, I don't understand what I see. I can only open the door part way. Something solid, cold, and white blocks its progress. The rope lifeline that leads to the woodshed is gone. That is no matter. Because my woodshed is also gone. Either that, or it's buried beneath a mountain's worth of snow.

Why the avalanche spared my little house, I do not know. But it has. And yet, it hardly feels benevolent. I do not feel grateful.

For a very long time, I do nothing but stare at the snow. Then I shut the door. I throw the deadbolt.

I will never open it again.

*

I use the last of the dying embers to light a cheap candle. The flame throws little light and even less heat. A couple of them on the hearth chase away the worst of the dark—if not the cold. Jatar is speaking to me now, urging me forward. Before the cold can steal all my rational thoughts, I scrawl *Crank the handle* on any surface I might chance to look at—the floor, the walls, the plastic tub that once held the blankets and clothes I stumble around in.

My fingers are black from the burnt bit of wood that was my makeshift pen. I use as little water as possible to wash, although this is from habit. I will run out before the water does.

"The storeroom," Jatar says. "You can navigate in the dark. I'll help you. Don't take a candle."

"All right." I push to standing.

"Go straight back and then to your left."

"My left." I don't say it as a question, but that's what it is.

"That's the hand with the burn." He never scolds, even when my words come out stupid.

"On the shelf, above your head, there will be another bin of blankets and things to keep you warm."

Halfway inside the storeroom, my mind blanks. Everything is dark, but Jatar's voice echoes behind me.

"A few more steps, dear girl. Just a few."

How he knows what I need to do, I can't say. Perhaps, before the avalanche, I spoke of these things. Yes. I nod to myself. I did. I told him where everything was and now he's telling me. I lug the bin from the shelf and emerge into the dim light of the main room.

My movement causes one of my candles to sputter. It gutters and dies. Maybe it's the cheap wax, but it sounds like someone drowning.

"Soshi? Are you there?"

"Yes, I'm here."

"That noise?"

"One of my candles," I say. "The flame went out."

"It sounded horrific."

"It sounded like someone's throat being slit."

Jatar's voice fills the speakers, but I don't understand him. His voice has a musical quality to it, as if he uses notes rather than words. But I recognize the tone.

He is scolding me.

At last he comes to himself, the notes fading into lyrics I understand.

"Soshi, please."

He doesn't call me *dear girl*, and I think that hurts more than anything else. That makes me rush to explain before the cold steals this piece of me as well.

"I said that because I know what it sounds like. I've heard it before. It's why I left the group. They weren't collecting children because they were kind. They were collecting children because they were hungry."

Jatar is silent.

"I ran away," I continue. "I'd rather die alone than be someone's dinner. I left the group, stopped following the train tracks, and found my mountain."

"I had no idea, dear girl, no idea. You've never … I mean, I didn't know."

"I don't like to think about it."

"Then we won't speak of it ever again. Go on, open the bin. There are warm things inside."

I pull the items out, one by one. They are heavy in my hands, thick wool coats that might weigh more than I do at this point. There are light things as well, down-filled jackets and sleeping bags that sprout tiny feathers when I squeeze them. At the very bottom, there is something furry and soft. I don't recognize it, and it isn't something you wear. It almost looks like...

"Jatar! I have a mouse!"

"Do you now?" He sounds amused.

"Yes! Did you ... did you find a way to send me a mouse?"

"I did, dear girl, I did."

"Is it my birthday?"

"I think it might be."

"I should have a can of peaches then."

"You should have two."

"Oh, I don't know if I could eat two whole cans." I am not as hungry as I used to be. Sometimes Jatar must bully me into eating.

"Try," he says now. "Pretend I'm there, and the second can is for me."

In the end, I manage to eat one and a half cans. This gives me energy to make tea. The drink heats my throat, my stomach, and for a few moments, I can pretend I feel warm.

"You know what you should do, now that you have a mouse?" he asks.

"What?" I am amazed that there's something I can do, so he has my full attention.

"Build a nest, one you can share with it. You can keep each other warm."

I do as he says, piling the heavy coats along the floor and against the wall near the hearth. I move the radio within arm's reach. I can keep the candles lit from here. I curl into the blankets and pull the mouse to me.

"Would you mind," I ask, "if I called him Jatar?"

"I would be honored."

*

*Crank the handle.*

I know the words mean something, something important. I know there's something I must do, but can't remember. When the last of the candles dies and the dark erases the words, it's almost a relief.

I pull my mouse to me, cuddle him against my neck. He is so soft.

"Don't be scared," I whisper.

Because he is scared, of the dark, of the cold so sharp it feels like a knife's blade. I dig us further into our nest.

"Close your eyes, Jatar. Go to sleep."

I shut my eyes. The sound of a voice pricks my ears, but I think this voice is in my head, not in my house. It is a rich voice, amused and musical. When I try, I can make this voice laugh.

And in that laughter, there is warmth.

***

It's the silence in the end that's the worst, when Soshi's voice no longer fills my shuttlecraft, when I know she's alone, in the dark. She has her mouse, I tell myself; she has her version of Jatar. She is not alone. This thought offers nothing, not even a cold sort of comfort.

Earth was never in my sector of responsibility. Before Soshi, I knew very little of it, just that it was another small, life-bearing planet. Enough small, life-bearing planets implode on our watch that one more hardly makes a difference.

Except, of course, when it does.

As always, the jolt takes me unaware, throws me into the control panel. Pain shoots along my extremities. The grind of metal on metal follows and what sounds like a ripping. I brace against the floor, the craft shuddering beneath me. I count to three.

And then it ends. Everything is solid around me. Everything is as it should be. Everything is the same.

"Hello?"

Including Soshi.

"Hello? Hello? Is anyone there? Can you hear me? I would like to talk to you."

Why my communications system picks up her transmission, I don't know. It hasn't failed to yet, just as the crash never fails to surprise me, never fails to injure. I push to stand, then fall back. I strain and stretch, managed to press a button, call out a few words, although they are rough. My memories are intact, but each time, I must relearn her language. In those precious moments, it is easy to lose her.

"Hello! Hello! Are you there? Can you hear me? Hello?"

I can't find the will to move. I'm not certain I have it in me to live through this again—I've lost track of the number of times.

"Please. Talk to me."

If I lie here and soak in my own juices, what good will that do? But if I claw to stand, lock onto her frequency, what good will *that* do?

Every time is different. Every time … breaks me a little more. My sigh comes across the frequency, changes her thought or her footfall or something, and I open up another vista into her soul. Just when I thought I knew all of Soshi's trials, she tells me of shaking bones from a dead woman's boots and those who collect children in order to eat them.

I spend this time between her first call and that last, desperate one deciding. Earlier, I researched. While Earth never was in my sector, our information is complete, and what's stored on the shuttlecraft is more than I'll ever need. Quite against my will, I've become the foremost expert on hypothermia in humans.

When the end is near, I coax her into burrowing, better that than paradoxical undressing. I know when the avalanche will strike and her best chance to survive it. Once she stepped outside and it took her. I listened to icy silence until the battery on the radio finally died.

I have a complete mental inventory of her storeroom. What she finds in the bottom of that bin, I'm never certain. A child's toy? A fur-lined glove? A hat meant for an infant, perhaps, with whimsical ears.

"Hello? Are you there? I think I heard you last night. Well, it's always night here. I mean, before. I heard you before."

My strength returns, but so does my resolve not to answer. Does it matter, one way or another, if I'm there for her? Must I bear witness? She dies. She always dies. Once, I'd like that not to happen.

"Is there anyone there?" Her words are slow, deliberate, plaintive. "Should I change frequencies?"

Her question holds humor, as if she recognizes that it's a somewhat ridiculous thing to ask. The first time I heard it, I launched myself to my feet, smashed into the control panel, and opened a communications channel. Now, I hesitate, but thoughts cloud my mind. She will not find her mouse without me. She will step into that avalanche.

She will die alone.

I propel myself off the floor. I land with a crack against the control panel. I still ooze, and I coat the surface with what can only be described as slime, at least in human terms.

"No." It's more of a cough than a word, but it crosses space and time and opens her up to me.

"No?"

Her voice is filled with so much hope, choking out a reply is almost impossible. The panel is such a mess that establishing a permanent link is, also, almost impossible.

"Don't … don't change the frequency … there's a good girl. Hold tight, I'm having some technical difficulties, but I'm here."

I'm always here.

In a manner of speaking.

"In a Manner of Speaking" originally appeared in *Selfies from the End of the World: Historical Accounts of the Apocalypse*.

# Moon, Flower, Sword, Kendra

by Tom Wharton

Walking home one evening from a dance at his high school, a boy discovers he has acquired a moon.

It is simply there, after not being there ever before. The boy stops in his tracks and stares. The shining disk hangs in space a few inches from his forehead, so that he has to lift his gaze slightly to look at it. The moon is full, chalk white, and about as big as a medium-sized marble. And in fact that's what he thinks it is at first: the beautiful pearlescent shooter that was the pride of his collection when he was eight and that he lost long ago. But this is no marble. The sphere's unmistakably lunar surface resembles that of everyone's Moon, the one in the night sky: pocked with craters and scarred with troughs and ridges.

At first the boy thinks the moon is simply hanging suspended in the air, motionless. Then he realizes that it's moving, with the same mysterious creeping swiftness as *the* Moon. He stands very still and watches it pass in front of one of the streetlights down the road ahead of him. For the briefest moment there's a black disc and a reddish corona as the tiny sphere eclipses the glow of the sodium-vapour lamp, then the light flares out again as the moon moves on in its silent path.

The boy reaches up to touch this unexpected visitor, to confirm it's actually here, then pulls his hand back. What if he disturbs its orbit and sends it hurtling away from him? He doesn't want that to happen, although he can't say why.

It's a cold evening, with a sharp wind. The boy hurries on, eager to get home where it's warm and he is waited for. He's relieved but also troubled to see that the moon comes with him.

At home the cat hisses at this new thing and runs off to hide. The boy's parents marvel at the moon's beauty, but his father also goes online to make sure this isn't something to be concerned about. He finds a physics website that says people sometimes attract exotic matter from other regions of the universe and nobody has figured out why, as yet, but that in most cases there are no adverse effects.

That night the boy lies back in bed and gazes up at his shining companion (made of exotic enough matter, apparently, to pass unhindered through his pillow and blankets). He studies the moon's features, its rills and domes and mountain ranges, the starburst rays around its craters, the dark grey medallions of its ancient lava flows which long-ago astronomers mistook for seas. Gazing up he feels like a sea himself, as if some deepness in him he hadn't known existed is being drawn like a tide by the moon's gentle pull. He tries to figure out whether the darker scars and patches make the shape of anything. Maybe a squinting, pock-marked face (he has to squint himself to make anything like a face appear), or a hand holding out a bouquet of roses to someone who isn't there, or a child waving goodbye to a lost balloon.

When the boy gets tired of looking at the moon he thinks about the dance earlier in the evening. He didn't ask any girls to dance and none asked him. His friends, who hadn't danced with anyone either, were acting like idiots and getting on his nerves, so he decided to leave. Outside on the steps someone called his name. It was a girl he hardly knew, standing in a little huddle on the lawn with her friends. His heart lurched. He secretly liked her, but had always felt a vague hostility toward her too, because she hung out with the tough, wild crowd, a group he wasn't part of and never would be. Warily he went over to her. The girl had been drinking, he could see that. She repeated his name, drawing the syllables out, like the two of them were old pals who hadn't seen each other in ages, then she asked him why he was leaving so early. He told her the dance was boring and he was going home.

Not until you dance with me you're not, she said. She took him suddenly by the hands and swung around and around with him while her friends laughed. After a few spins he let go and walked away with a shrug, as if it was no big deal.

Goodbye, the girl called after him, saying his name over and over, like the refrain of a song.

It seemed to him then that something decisive had just happened. He felt more solid to himself somehow. More real, as if until this moment he had only been a shadowy background character in someone else's dream.

Not long after that the moon had appeared.

The boy's new satellite does not improve things at school. People point and ask rude questions. This one mean kid with pimples calls him "Moony" a few times but thankfully it doesn't catch on. The only person who takes a real interest is his science teacher. She is convinced the moon has to be more than a random event that might have happened to anyone.

There's something special about you, his science teacher tells him. I have a hunch your life is going to turn out like no one else's.

*

He gets to know the moon's luminous face as well as his own. It's too close to look at through binoculars or a telescope, so he uses a magnifying glass. The idea comes to him that he might be able to see its dark side by standing before the bathroom mirror when the moon's orbit brings it directly in front of him. All he sees reflected in the glass when he tries this, however, is a small, inky shadow that blots out part of his own face. Moonlight is a borrowed radiance, he knows. Wherever the light is coming from that gives his moon both a dark and a bright side, it's not from anywhere around here. His experiment with the mirror provides no clues, and only leaves him wondering if there's a side of himself, too, that he will never quite be able to see.

He names the moon's most prominent lava basins after people he secretly likes. The Sea of Julie. The Sea of Kamala. The Sea of Lucas. The moon itself he gives the name of the girl who danced with him on the lawn. He knows he will never tell anyone about these names, least of all her. Unless.

He is going to ask her out, he decides. He will go right up to her at her locker between classes and ask her out. Girls from her faction never date boys from his. He knows that. But he is the boy with the moon. The moon he's given *her* name. And after all, if the science teacher is right about him, then maybe *she* is how his life will turn out like no one else's.

Every time the girl opens her mouth to speak, flowers come out. Most of the time only a single blossom, but sometimes they come spilling out in bright, colourful bunches. All kinds of flowers, too. Daffodils, daisies, red clover. Carnations, tulips, asters, geraniums. The occasional rose. Tiny star-shaped flowers she doesn't even know the names of. Now and then a flamboyant orchid, sultry with dew.

Thorns from the roses scratch her lips. Petals get stuck between her teeth. Even when she isn't talking bees follow her around, which makes other people flee. An ever-changing array of floral scents—fragrant, musky, lurid—fill her head all day and even at night, giving her disturbing dreams, like the one in which she slowly peels off all her clothing in public and sprawls naked on lawns and across the warm hoods of cars, letting everyone ogle and laugh and even touch her wherever they please.

It wasn't always like this. When she was a kid she spoke like everyone else. Then around the time she got to high school something changed, she couldn't say what, or why. She would know the answer to a question the teacher asked in class, or she would have something important to tell her friends, and instead of what she wanted to say, out popped these stupid, embarrassing flowers.

There's someone else at her school with a weird thing: a boy with his own moon. Maybe they could be friends, she thinks, but instead they avoid each other, the fellow condemned.

This one jerk with bad acne calls her Vegetable Patch, and then just Veg, which doesn't really make sense, but still hurts. And there's a girl she secretly likes, too, in one of her classes. Kendra. The girl who speaks flowers has never dared talk to Kendra, but watches her so often and with such discreet but careful attention that she can replay in her head, any time she wishes, the easy swagger of Kendra's walk, her skeptical head tilt when chatting with her friends, the feline way she stretches up on tiptoe to put her books on the top shelf of her locker. Kendra is loud and brash and acts like she doesn't care about anything, but she smiled at the girl one time in a way that showed deep down she was actually really nice.

Every time the girl musters the courage to speak to Kendra, she remembers the flowers, and keeps her distance. There is just too much at stake.

After she graduates and moves out on her own she imagines things will get better, that people will be mature and understanding. They aren't. Meeting someone new for the first time is a trial, a humiliation. And her old friends are caught up now in their adult lives. To them the flowers are so *high school*. On occasion she meets someone new who thinks the flower trick is impressive, if useless. They'll pester her to say other things, more practical things, like tomatoes, or coins, or live ammunition. She becomes quiet and reclusive, avoids conversations, but everywhere she goes people expect her to speak, they insist she say what they want to hear, and mostly what they want to hear is their own opinions echoed back to them. They are not expecting nor do they have any use for these mute, innocent blossoms that seem an obscure rebuke to anyone who uses real words to talk about real things.

After a while most people just leave her alone. Which is fine. She is good with computers and not long after finishing high school she finds a job that can be done from home, as a tech support person for a major online travel agency. So she just keeps doing that, and rarely goes out. This botanical disability, as her supervisor calls it, doesn't adversely affect the quality or efficiency of her work. He can even promote it as proof that the company proudly supports the differently abled.

Driving home one night from another melancholy dinner with her aging parents, she gets caught in an early winter blizzard. In a breathtakingly short time there is nothing to see through the window but fat wet flakes of flurrying snow. She slows the car to a crawl, cursing, and finally pulls over to wait it out. Enclosed in a hushed, swirling cocoon, she feels as if she has strayed out of the real world into an unsuspected district of ghosts. To prove to herself she's still here, and still herself, she speaks her own name. Instead of the familiar syllables out drops a small, pale, almost translucent blossom. Its limp, greyish-white petals are laced with faint blueish veins. Later, after much scrolling through a dizzying garden of floral images, she finds the most likely match: henbane. Which doesn't even grow here, as far as she knows, and sounds like something witches sprinkle into their potions. She burns the flower in an oven pan on her apartment balcony.

Maybe, she considers, after she's browsed on from flower identification sites and stumbled into the Web's inexhaustible bounty of real-life horror stories, maybe she really doesn't have it so bad.

Not like the man who speaks razorblades.

Or the woman who speaks spiders.

*

The young man with acne scars spends most of his time slouched in front of the television, a game controller gripped tightly in his hands.

He is between jobs.

Once a week his mother comes over to his apartment to bring him meals and clean up after him. When she does she tells him he has so much to give. He should get out there and show everyone what he can do. The man nods and says yep, I'm gonna do that, Mom, not taking his eyes off the screen. His mother says good for you, then she goes back to washing the man's dirty dishes and gathering up his dirty laundry.

One night after the man climbs into bed he hears a faint ringing in his right ear. He lies there for a long time, fixated on the noise and thinking this must be one of those odd things your body does every so often that go away after a while, never to return. But the ringing doesn't go away. If anything it gets louder. The man tries yawning and clearing his throat. He shakes his head back and forth, up and down. He thumps his temple with his hand. The ringing goes on ringing.

The man climbs angrily out of bed and picks up where he left off his current game, upping the difficulty level from Blood-spattered Grind to Exalted Madness. The ringing goes on, keeping him from sinking out of the world and into the game like he normally does without a thought. And now, even worse, the ringing has acquired a rhythm, a sharp, relentless *ting TING ting TING*, like metal being tapped deliberately on metal, that nearly drives him frantic.

After a miserable, sleepless night he heads to a walk-in clinic first thing in the morning. The doctor looks in the young man's right ear and says *Huh. Never seen this before.* Carefully wielding a small pair of tweezers the doctor pulls something out of the young man's ear. *Ow ow ow*, the young man says.

The doctor holds up what she's found.

A tiny sword. About the length of a pinky finger.

Will you look at that, the young man says.

The ringing in his ear is gone.


He takes the sword home with him and spends a long time marveling at the bright elfin blade, the barely-perceptible stipple of the dark leather hilt. The point looks sharp, but when he pokes it into his palm experimentally the blade flexes, hardly bites at all. Just a little sting.

For some reason, just then, he remembers a girl he went to high school with. The one who threw up flowers whenever she tried to talk. He'd forgotten all about her until just now. How he'd wished back then for something like she had, the thing that made her like nobody else. Sure, probably not flowers, but *something*. He'd wanted it so bad he was cruel to her, called her awful names. It's obvious to him now why he did this. There were times he'd thought about killing himself, because of his skin condition. He doesn't think that way so much anymore. The video games have worked pretty well keeping those sorts of thoughts at bay.

The young man pushes away these unpleasant memories. He swings the sword slowly back and forth, whispering *swish swish*, then puts it down again. He looks at his game controller perched on the arm of the sofa. It needs charging. He doesn't get up to charge it. Later he puts the sword in an empty matchbox and tucks it away in a drawer, in back of his few mismatched items of cutlery, then goes to bed.

The next morning the young man prints off a sheaf of resumes and heads out to look for a job. He has no luck the first day, but when he gets home, instead of playing video games he packs up his gaming system and posts it for sale online. He goes out job-hunting all that week, and every evening when he returns home, footsore but happy, he takes out the sword. He turns it over in his fingers, admiring the blade's flashing silver gleam. Sometimes he pretends he's fighting tiny monsters with it. He whispers *swish swish* as he sweeps the sword back and forth, cutting down evil things. Then he feels foolish, and tucks the sword away again in its matchbox.

The man's mother comes over. She's startled to find the house tidied up and her son sitting at the kitchen table looking through job postings on the internet. You should take a break from that, she says to him. You don't want to do too much all at once.

Okay, Mom, the man says.

There is nothing for her to clean, so she goes home.

At last the man finds a job, as a waiter. He enjoys the work, and it shows. People like him. They tip him generously. The man buses home tired but content most nights. He's helped bring a little joy into people's lives, by treating each one of them, while they're at the restaurant, like the most important person in the world. He puts his tip money in a jar and for the first time in his life thinks about a possible future.

At lunchtime one day an unhappy-looking young woman comes into the restaurant alone. Catching sight of her from the kitchen the young man realizes she's someone who went to his high school. He doesn't want to serve her because she might recognize him and he isn't that person anymore. But it can't be helped, his co-worker called in sick and he's the only waiter on shift right now. He goes over to her table. The woman's blank look tells him she has no idea who he is, or was. When he asks her what she would like she says, To not be a fuck-up.

I can relate, he says. The young woman laughs.

She returns almost every day that week, and by the end of the week he feels pretty sure it's mostly to see him. Finally they exchange phone numbers and begin to date.

In time the young man becomes assistant manager of the restaurant, then manager, and eventually owner. He transforms the place into one of the most popular and highly regarded dining establishments in town. Eventually he and the young woman get married and move in together.

One day while she's cleaning out their overstuffed cutlery drawer, the man's wife finds the matchbox. She shakes the sword out of the box and brings it to her husband.

What's this? she asks.

He grins. He hasn't thought about the sword in ages, and feels a little gush of gratitude to see it again.

It's what brought me to you, the man tells his wife. Or you to me.

After he relates the story to her, his wife buys a small jewelry box with a plush, purple interior to keep the sword in. She places it high up on a shelf in the kitchen.

The years go by and life is busy and fulfilling. One day their little boy gets a chair and climbs up on the kitchen counter to find out what's in the box. He takes the sword to his father and asks if he can play with it. The man says yes, but to be careful. The sword isn't really all that sharp but you never know.

When he remembers days later and asks where the sword is, his son doesn't know. The man searches for it everywhere but never finds it.

He's sad about this, but with time, and because there are much bigger heartaches to come, and yet so much in life to be thankful for, he forgets about the sword.

When the man is dying his family gathers around his hospital bed. His children, grown up now, have come from near and far. The woman who was his wife comes too, with her wife, who to his own surprise and after some difficult years he's come to think of with fondness as one of his best friends.

His family tells him he is a good man and a wonderful father and he says goodbye to them all.

He knows he is dying, but it isn't what he expected. Has anything ever been? First everybody in the room gets quieter and further and further away, until he can no longer see them and he is all alone. Then he sees a small moving figure coming toward him over the white bedsheet, like someone trudging through deep snow. It's a little person in bright silver armor, carrying a tiny sword.

*His* sword.

There it is. How had he forgotten it? Where had he left it?

When the little person in armor gets closer, holding out the sword with the hilt forward, the man reaches out his hand. And now the sword is bigger, or he is smaller, because the sword fits perfectly in his grip like a real full-sized sword. The blade flashes, as good as new.

The little person in armor bows and walks away.

The man isn't in his hospital bed anymore. He is standing on a windswept, snowy plain with the sword in his hand.

The man swings the sword back and forth. *Swish, swish*, he whispers. Then he starts walking.

*

The woman comes to her fifteen-year high school reunion reluctantly. She stayed away from the ten-year reunion: even though she'd mostly overcome the flower problem by then, there were still rare but unpredictable moments when a daisy or a dandelion slipped out. But she hasn't had an episode for quite a while now and felt it was time to see these people again. To show them she is just like them.

She's surprised by what happened to the pimply kid who mocked her so relentlessly. He owns his own restaurant now, a place she has heard great things about but hasn't visited yet. But more than that, something fundamental has changed in him. She feels a quiet warmth and goodwill radiating from him that, despite her desire to hold a bitter but oh so righteous grudge, ends up winning her over.

I'm so sorry for the way I treated you, he tells her. The truth is, I wanted to be like you. I mean, you know, like nobody else in the world. I just didn't know how to tell you that.

She nods, and a painful lump forms in her throat, but she doesn't dare reply. For the first time in years she knows for certain that if she speaks it will be in flowers, and he might take that as a taunt, or a rebuke.

Just as surprising as his transformation is the fact that he's married to Kendra, the girl she had a secret crush on all those years ago. Kendra has changed, too. Or rather, the kindness she felt hiding behind Kendra's bad-girl act is now there for all to see. She has become who she's always been.

As they greet one another with a hug the woman feels an old, carefully-buried longing welling up. How she yearned to be close to that kindness back then, to have it bestowed on her, and only her. And how much, she is startled now to discover, she still wishes for that.

The woman and Kendra sit together at a table and catch up on each other's lives and those of their classmates. Kendra is on the reunion organizing committee and has kept up with what people are doing, has gleaned intriguing bits and pieces of their lives. Trying not to be obvious the woman points out people she remembers only vaguely, or not at all, and asks Kendra about them.

What about him? she asks, inclining her head at someone across the banquet hall she hasn't noticed until now, a balding man with a cold, scornful look on his face, standing just inside the entrance. The man has a beautiful ring of faintly shining dust encircling his head, like Saturn's.

Kendra looks shocked.

He told us he wasn't coming, she says.

The woman realizes the man with the ring was the boy who had his own moon.

Oh he was such a sweetheart, she says, and along with her words a small white peony pops out that she quickly hides under her hand. What happened to him? she asks.

Kendra smiles, but it's a pained smile. She looks down and plucks at the tablecloth.

I did, she says.


The man with the ring like Saturn's goes around the room and shakes hands with people and shares memories and even smiles once or twice. But just as quickly as it appears the smile falls away. He is very aware of the woman he named his moon after, sitting at a table on the other side of the banquet hall. He knows that if she hasn't noticed him yet she will soon enough. It's the only reason he finally decided to show his face tonight.

Yes, he thinks bitterly and not for the first time, his science teacher was right. His life has turned out like no one else's. Whose doesn't? That doesn't mean it has turned out *well*. Nothing has ever been easy. Nothing has ever turned out the way he hoped. And maybe none of that is her fault, maybe no one's to blame, but he wants her to see what's become of his moon, and remember how she hurt him, and feel bad. A few more minutes, just to be sure she's seen him, then he can leave and that will be the end of it.

Then the woman's husband, who used to be that nasty kid with acne, comes up and shakes his hand, says it's good to see him, and really seems to mean it. The husband invites the man to sit with them, and to his own surprise he goes. There's another woman at the table with *her*, someone he vaguely recalls suffering some sort of embarrassing problem in high school, though he can't remember what it was. He shakes hands with her, and with the woman he named his moon after, and sits down. It seems certain this will be painfully awkward, and at first it is, but eventually everyone begins to talk more freely, and even to joke and laugh, and he realizes he doesn't know any of these people any more, if he ever did.

The lights are dimmed for dancing, and the man's ring shines more brightly. From beneath its pale glow he looks out at the beaming faces around the table and they seem to him like celestial objects reflecting their own unseen sources of light. The odd thought comes to him that they've all been orbiting one another, near or far, for such a long time, and this is—what do they call it?—a rare planetary alignment. He thinks *fifteen years*, which now seems more like a distance than a time, and just like that he sees how pathetic and futile his little revenge plot is.

A popular song from their high school days starts thumping from the speakers, one of those monster hits everybody loved. The others get up to dance and invite him to join them. He isn't quite done feeling sorry for himself, so he tells them maybe in a while. He sits and watches the others dancing and having a good time, and he reaches up like he sometimes does when he's preoccupied, catching a little of his ring's fine glittering dust on his fingertips. The lunar matter has become less exotic over the years, it seems. He looks at the dust a moment (one day, if he keeps this up, there will be no ring left) then with a puff of breath sends it away, a spiralling, dissipating cloud that discloses no meaningful pattern at all.

*

Kendra drops back into her folding chair and brushes the hair out of her eyes. Her head is whirling and she's going to regret these shoes come morning. She's probably had too much to drink, too. She smiles at the man across the table from her, the boy whose dreams she took in her hands and thoughtlessly tossed aside. Her husband is across the room now, busy bringing a smile to someone else's face. She feels her phone quiver in her purse, which is on the floor, touching her ankle. She has a quick look: the babysitter checking in. The kids are in bed, all is well.

A woman sits down beside her, a shy, lovely woman whose hair has come a little loose now. The girl she always wished to know but who slipped away from her back then, leaving only stray petals. Something has begun here, like a story's about to be told to her that she's never heard. Lights drift over them from the old glitter ball she helped put up earlier in the evening.

You never knew what life was going to bring you. When she was a little girl and lived in another town her father left and her mother bought her a dog. She loved that dog. Their favourite game was when she would toss a rubber ball onto the roof of the house and it would bounce back down and her dog would try to catch it when it dropped off the edge. The dog never knew exactly where the ball was going to be when it dropped. He would whine and jump around frantically until the thing he was so desperate for suddenly appeared, then he would make a mad dash for it. Just like the rest of us, she thought years later, after she'd left her husband for another woman and was tracing with amazement the unforeseeable road she had taken through life. One time she threw the ball really hard on purpose, so that it sailed over the roof and into the front yard. The dog somehow knew it wasn't coming back and tore off after it. A moment later she heard a squeal and the screech of brakes. She walked slowly around the house to the front yard. She already knew and she didn't want to see, but she had to see. A postal delivery truck was parked wrong, half on the sidewalk in front of her house. The delivery man was coming up the front walk, crying, carrying her dog in his arms, like a parcel she had never been told was on its way to her door.

# Contributors

Janet Barrow is a Minnesota raised, Hudson Valley educated, writer of fiction. She believes, first and foremost, in the generative, restorative, and transformative powers of fiction. After two years in Lima, Peru, she recently moved to Chicago, where in addition to her fiction work, she writes about linguistic phenomena for Alta Language Services. Her work has appeared in *Adelaide Magazine*.

Elizabeth Browne has a degree in Japanese and has lived and worked in both South Korea and Japan. She earned her MFA from Emerson College. Her short stories and essays have appeared in *Unstuck, Minnetonka Review*, and *Clare*. She lives in San Francisco.

Christopher Fox lives in Brooklyn, and received his MFA from Hunter College. His work has previously appeared in *The Kenyon Review* and *3Elements Review*. When he's not writing stories, he's helping clients tell theirs as a speechwriter at West Wing Writers.

Alice Hatcher's work has appeared in *Alaska Quarterly Review, The Beloit Fiction Journal, Notre Dame Review, Mon-*

*keybicycle*, and *Fiction International*, among other journals. Her novel *The Wonder That Was Ours* won Dzanc Books 2017 Fiction Prize and was long listed for the Center for Fiction's 2018 First Novel Award. Hatcher's work can be found at alice-hatcher.com.

Alexander Jones has short fiction and poetry appearing in Akashic Books, *Babbling of the Irrational*, *Crack the Spine*, and *DASH*, among other publications. His nonfiction was recently anthologized by 2Leaf Press. He has a BA in English/Creative Writing and is pursuing a second BA in History. He works as a metal fabricator and lives in New Jersey.

Larry Malchow's story "Trapped" was a semi-finalist in *The New Guard Literary Review* writing contest for 2018 and will appear in Volume VII. He is also a published poet and essayist.

Sara Ramey is an MFA candidate at the University of Arkansas and the recipient of fellowships intended to sponsor young writers. She reviews literature for several magazines, including the recently inaugurated *Arkansas International*, and volunteers with WITS, a program that introduces public school students to poetry.

Sara Daniele Rivera is a Cuban/Peruvian writer, artist, educator, and translator from Albuquerque, New Mexico. Her poetry and speculative fiction have appeared in *The Loft Anthology*, *Origins Journal*, *DIALOGIST*, *Storyscape Journal*, *Circuits & Slippers*, and elsewhere. She was awarded a 2017 St. Botolph's Emerging Artist Award in Literature.

Sara is currently working on a fantasy novel, a book of poetry, and on translating the work of Peruvian poet Blanca Varela.

Charity Tahmaseb has slung corn on the cob for Green Giant and jumped out of airplanes (but not at the same time). She's worn both Girl Scout and Army green. These days, she writes fiction and works as a technical writer. Her short speculative fiction has appeared in *Deep Magic*, *Escape Pod*, and *Cicada*.

Thomas Wharton's novels and stories have been published in Canada, the US, the UK, France, Germany, Italy, Japan, and other countries. His collection of magic realist fiction, *The Logogryph*, won the 2005 Writers' Guild of Alberta Award for Short Fiction, was nominated for the Sunburst Award for Canadian Fantasy, and short-listed for the International Dublin Literary Award. He teaches creative writing at the University of Alberta in Edmonton.